BRADD CHAMBERS

SOMEONE ELSE'S LIFE

BRADD CHAMBERS

BRADD CHAMBERS

Someone Else's Life
Copyright © Bradd Chambers 2017
Published in 2017 by Bradd Chambers

BRADD CHAMBERS

For my mum,
Who fuelled my love for books.

BRADD CHAMBERS

CHAPTER 1:

I rub my thumb over the smooth cold blade. Something about it relaxes me. It shouldn't, of course, but it does. I love the feel of it on my skin. It's been months since I found it. Lying unused and unwanted on the grass in the park. I'm itching to use it. To sink it into the stomach of one of my oblivious victims.

Someone who laughed at me. Someone who made my life hell. Someone who doesn't understand how good they've got it. No, someone nothing like me. They don't know how it feels.

Placing the knife back into my hoody pocket, I look up and down the street again. The darkness engulfs the old road, which was once the quickest way into town before that new bridge was built. Now, it's mostly deserted. Nothing but litter and graffiti and untrimmed hedges. I love being here at this time of night. The distant hum of the town centre. The zooming of cars, nothing but tiny specs of light, echoing my loneliness out here. Sometimes one passes by, headlights shining over me sitting on the bench. But the majority of the drivers barely glance my way. Too busy with their own perfect little lives.

A tattered rat from the bushes scurries over to the overflowing bin across the street from me. I hear its squeaks of delight as it rustles its whiskers into a crumpled Burger King bag. It's still too early for the rubbish men to come. The rat has its pick of what it wants now, whilst everyone else is absent. Feasting on what it likes before the hustle and bustle of everyday life. A bit like myself. The rat's silhouette is painted on the dull red bricks of the wall behind, making it look huge. Demonic even, as the dull street light flickers on and off.

A cold wind cuts my neck as I shrink my head back into my hood. I may as well make my way back soon. Maybe tomorrow. Just maybe I'll have the courage. I didn't have a lot of choice tonight. Everyone that went past were either drunk groups, coming back from a night in the town, or muscled men out for a midnight jog. I was scared to even glance at the latter. But every time someone crossed my path, my heart was in my throat. Counting their steps as they drew nearer.

Three... Two... One... Then they were gone.

I almost got the courage to stand up and follow three girls. They were laughing and holding on to each other drunkenly. One would have had to have slipped away from the group at some point. That's when I would have got my chance. But how could I have explained myself if they had have asked me why I was following them? Physically shaking, and not just from the cold, my hands wouldn't have been able to do it.

Yeah, tomorrow. I'll try again tomorrow. Standing up abruptly, I watch the rat retreating back into the shadows of the bushes. It's silhouette, once unstoppable, shrinking down to size until it has disappeared completely. Back into its hiding place. Disturbed only by me.

"You and me both, big fella," I laugh as I start back down the street, before my anonymity is spoiled by the daytime. Just like the rat's.

That's when I see her.

CHAPTER 2:

Gemma can't seem to shake the feeling that she's being followed. Despite looking behind her countless amount of times and flashing her phone light into the darkness to prove that she's alone, the hairs on the back of her neck still won't sit down. Even the shadows have shadows. She quickens her pace. Why didn't her dad just answer his phone? Now, with no money, she was forced to walk home at all hours of the morning. And through Promised Hill of all places.

Gemma was sure the hill was supposed to be prosperous once upon a time. The council had big plans for the hill, which was the main passage into the town after the motorway. Fancy houses, department stores and even a university campus was suggested. But, decades ago, when they ran out of money, the place went to squalor. Now it held the rougher members of Rong Valley's community. If there was a drug raid on the news, you could bet it would be in one of the dodgy looking flats Gemma had just walked past not five minutes earlier.

She's half way down David's Street by now, with a half mile between herself and the bridge into town. Her steps bouncing off the mouldy brick wall surrounding the local football pitch is all she can hear, before her phone pings in the silence. She opens up her Whatsapp group with a smile. The latest photo of Nichole Quigley has finally made the rounds of her mates, with more than five of them viewing and reacting to it.

'*Fat pig, why would you ware a bikini with a tummy like that? Lol,*' Chloe had just chipped in.

Gemma has a sudden surge of accomplishment that she was the first to screenshot the latest atrocity uploaded to Facebook.

'*Lol, ur right Chlo, why would you upload something lik-*'

Her latest rant is cut short with a twig crunching to her left, making her jump and drop her phone. As she snaps her head towards the source of the noise, she's met with a stretch of trees and shrubbery, two metres deep, separating David's Street from the back gardens of the houses in Winter Avenue/

Gemma clutches her hands to her chest, in a futile attempt to calm her beating heart, and gazes into the darkness, just about making out a high white garden fence. The moonlight barely breaks the canopy, but all she can see are the silhouettes of the trees and bushes fighting to break out into the road.

She swears and reaches down for her phone. For God's sake, it's face down on the pavement. She wipes the muck and tiny pebbles off the screen, but never makes it to inspecting whether it's smashed.

A blow to her side winds her and makes her fall on to the road, rolling a few times. Clambering up, she twists one arm around her back to massage the inevitable bruise and sticks her free arm out to lever herself onto her feet. Ready to run. But her attacker leaks from the darkness on top of her. She opens her mouth to scream, but the sound is lost as a blade bites bluntly into her stomach. She gurgles as the figure towering over her thrusts the weapon into her again and

13

again, but never in the same spot. Always a few inches apart. Making the sharp pain throb around her whole abdomen.

After the fourth time, the knife slides out of her, opening the flood gates to a fresh rush of blood. She leans her head back on the pavement and gazes up to see the last face she's sure she'll ever see in this world. But a black hood covers her assailant's features. With a sniff, they step over her and run back into the trees. She tries twisting her neck to see them retreat, but it hurts too much.

Gemma tries to scream again. To attract the attention of the surrounding houses. Help only feet away behind giant wooden barricades. But as she opens her mouth, the only thing to escape is a slither of blood which runs idly down her chin.

CHAPTER 3:

The principal's office. A place most students hate to be. Every time you did something wrong, you shook with fear when your teacher marched you down the stretched corridor towards the door of the demon. You cried and screamed and squirmed to get out of the angry teacher's firm grip. But sooner or later, you're through that fiery gate with nothing but the desk to welcome you. The scorching heat made you sweat freely as you stared at the back of the chair.

"James Kingston," the teacher spat venomously, her glasses ablaze with the reflection of the flames. The chair swivels around and you scream at the sight of the red devil in the smart suit, chuckling wickedly, considering your fate.

Okay, a bit over dramatic, but as a kid I always had a wild imagination. That's what it was like in primary school. Begging and bargaining with the teacher to take pity on me. The principal roaring at me as I sank into the seat in his office. My parent's disappointed faces that night at the dinner table. "Why can't you be more like your older brother?"

But once I left primary school, everything changed. I loved the principal's office. That's where I am now, in Mr Deans' office. He's my should-be-ex principal. I left this school in June, but I failed my last exam, so can't get into the uni I want. I cursed them when I found out and hung up the phone. Looking back now, I didn't do myself any favours reacting that way.

I've been in and out of this office all week trying to sort things out with different universities, but they're all the same. Deans reckons I have to repeat the year, therefore graduating secondary school when I'm twenty. As you can guess, I'm not essentially happy with the idea. The school's okay and the teachers are nice enough, once Mrs Reilly, the old fossil, retired last year. The only thing annoying me is that all of my friends are now at university without me. To be honest, I do admire Deans for trying his best and my fingers are still crossed that he can do something.

He stumbles in, half an hour late, typical. Greeting me with his huge signature smile, he throws his tacky briefcase down on the table, still scratch free after all these years. He sits down, sighs and starts swinging on his chair.

"It's not looking good, James," he starts and looks away from me, fidgeting uncomfortably. "No one will accept you without your pass in all three A Levels. I've been discussing your situation with the school board and they've agreed to let you stay on for a further year. But as well as your Maths, you'll have to take up two more subjects. It won't matter in the long run, but it's just so you can stay in school. Everyone in the sixth form must do at least three subjects. It's school policy."

I knew it was coming, but my stomach still drops. On top of having to spend the year with the bottom class, who I now regret not talking to in the past, I have to do two extra subjects I have no interest in? I hide my frown and struggle a smile. Thanking him, I stand up, making towards the door.

"James," Deans sighs. "Sit back down."

I pause, my hands on the door handle. I can just twist it and leave. Pretend I didn't hear him. Go to college and study there? Maybe get into uni next year, or a few years later? Take a year out? Work and don't bother studying? The road ahead is filled with side lanes and opportunities. After all, I've never been the conventional type.

But my respect for the principal makes me linger too long, so I turn around and sit back down, staring at my hands.

"Don't worry, James," Deans says. "You're still going to get to university. I promise. You're a bright kid. They did like your personal statement, but they just can't take you because of your grades. As long as you pass this year, you'll be out of here in no time. Think of it as a deferral year, or a year out. It doesn't matter about your other two subjects, as long as you pass your Maths, they're happy to accept you..."

He talks to me for a while longer and I must admit, he does cheer me up. When I leave the office, I'm in a relatively better mood, but still a bit annoyed. It'll be a very lonely year, but it would be far worse without Deans. He's the only reason I haven't decided to transfer schools to save myself the embarrassment. With no friends in the lower class, I say I'll be spending most of my time in his office.

I hop on the bus with the sea of uniforms I will undoubtedly have to wear again, come Monday morning. First years give me funny looks and a few people I'd know to see give me the usual awkward *'heys.'* Making my way to the back of the bus, I see a bunch of boys from the year below sitting in our seats. My eyebrows raise as I continue down the aisle towards them. What are they doing? Those are *our* seats. Everyone knows that. We had to wait until we were in our final year to get those seats, so they should...

Then it hits me. They *are* in their final year. They *do* have the right to sit there. None of my friends are here anymore. I cough slightly as my cheeks go red. One of the rougher looking ones gives me a good look up and down. His ginger curly hair looks like it hasn't been washed in a week, his ears wouldn't be out of place attached to the World Cup and his mouth is so clenched I wouldn't be surprised if he's been fed wasps for dinner for the majority of his life.

I sigh and retreat back to the front, plonking myself down beside a kid a few years below. Not an overly popular one at that, but obviously embarrassed enough to be sitting beside someone in a jacket and jeans. As he shuffles as close to the window as he can get, I roll my eyes. You'd think I was wearing a giant chicken costume the way he's reacting.

CHAPTER 4:

Walking down my street, I see Stacey sitting on my front doorstep. Although it's September, the weather likes to change from its normal drizzly dullness to a lovely two-week holiday as soon as the school bell rings. She looks so beautiful and radiant sitting beside the huge flowers my mum planted. Her blonde hair has been curled at the tips, my favourite. Her mini skirt shows those incredible legs and I get goose bumps staring at them.

Smiling, I start up the drive. After the day I've had, I'd love a big hug. As my shadow envelopes her, she takes off her sunglasses and I see her beautiful, big blue eyes sparkling up at me. As I get closer, I halt. Her eyes are sparkling with tears, not admiration for my arrival home. And the look they're giving me instantly tells me that I'm in trouble.

The smile fades from my face, but I keep quiet and offer her a hand up. Her eyes are like daggers, so I put my hands back in my pocket, cough and start up the steps to my door. I open it and look around. She's still staring up at where I stood seconds before. Shifting uncomfortably, I ask her if she's coming in. She stares a while longer, then tuts, stands up and walks straight past me and up the stairs. Rolling my eyes and closing the door, I trot into the kitchen. Mum smiles at me coming and asks about my latest meeting with Deans.

When I finish my story, Mum's smile has dropped and she comes over and hugs me. She gives me the same old *'no distractions from your friends will help you pass the exam,'* and *'the year will fly in'* crap. Half way through the lecture, Stacey walks into the room, takes one look at us, sniffs and walks over to pour herself a drink. Mum sighs, pulls away and ruffles my hair, sensing Stacey's bad mood. She checks on dinner in the oven before withdrawing into the living room. Stacey's sitting at the table staring out of the window and tapping her fingers impatiently.

"What's wrong with you?" I question nervously.

"What were you talking about?" she spits.

"About school. I have to go back for a year. Deans was-"

"I heard my name."

My eyebrows raise and lip curls. Not once did we mention her name.

"What are you talking about? I never said-"

"Bitching about me when I'm just upstairs. That's real mature. I think you're forgetting that your room is just above us. I heard *every word* you said."

I fight the urge to tell her that directly above the kitchen is the bathroom, on the other side of the landing from my room.

"So, you have to stay behind a year? You never told me this," Stacey's eyes narrow. "Come crying to your mum but you can't say two words to me? Honestly don't understand why I both-"

"Stacey, you marched up the stairs as soon as we got here. You're clearly in a bad mood, why would I make it worse?"

"What, so you were just never going to tell me?"

"What? Of course I was, but I was going to wait until you were in a better mood-"

"Some girlfriend I am if you can't even tell me what's happening in your life. Especially big things such as this."

"Well, if you didn't look at me like a piece of dog shit on your shoe, then maybe I would've told you."

"Right, whatever. I'm going back upstairs-"

"No, go home if you're going to be in a mood like this. Whatever's wrong with you, it's got nothing to do with me. I want to be able to go up to my room later without worrying about an argument starting because you're in there. Just leave now, I'm really annoyed and upset that I can't get into uni and-"

"Not my fault."

My hand slaps my forehead.

"I never said it-"

"Maybe if you had've tried a little harder in Maths class instead of sitting chatting to Charlotte."

I drag my hand down my face and stare at her through the gaps in my fingers. Her eyes haven't moved from the window.

"Charlotte?"

She mumbles her agreement.

"Charlotte Jenkins?" I mutter, rage building.

She shrugs her shoulders and continues to stare out of the window. Despite the argument we're having, the look on her face has remained so calm. She looks like she could be staring at a pony grazing in the garden. That's what pisses me off. That's when I explode.

"Charlotte fucking Jenkins sat beside me in Maths class because the fucking teachers made us sit in alphabetical order," I scream.

I hear the TV volume in the living room decrease significantly. But I don't care. I've snapped.

"How many times do we have to have this fucking argument?"

She opens her mouth to protest.

"No, don't say a fucking word. As usual, I've had a completely shit day and you've managed to make it worse. Bringing Charlotte into this. She has fuck all to do with it. How old is this argument? Eh? Two years now, nearly. Get a fucking grip, Stacey."

Mum has come in to calm me down and Dad's head has peaked around from the living room door, but I'm beyond reasoning. Not even they can stop me when I'm like this.

"You always bring up stupid arguments when you have nothing else to say. Just get out of my fucking house. Now!"

Stacey stares at me, mouth open, tears in her eyes. She lets out a cry and storms across the room, slamming the back door. The window pane visibly shakes as we watch her run across the grass. I sigh and start to set the table. Keeping myself busy to control the anger. Ignoring my parents staring at me and the shaking of my hands as I throw the knives and forks on top of the dinner placemats.

This happens constantly. Stacey's mood swings put such a strain on our relationship. And on me. She's hard work, I'm not going to lie. One minute she's the most beautiful girl I know. But the next? The monster is released behind her pretty image. We've been together for over two years now, but every time I want to break up with her, I think about the Stacey that I love. Gorgeous, carefree and happy.

But she's got a darker side to her. A side I can't stand. She's insecure, jealous, controlling... Everything that is wrong with a relationship. She loves arguing with me. Sometimes I let her argue with herself and just ignore her. She'll tire herself out eventually and come crawling back. But sometimes I just can't take it. Like tonight. Sometimes I just completely crack. I hate getting walked over and treated like that, especially when I've done nothing wrong.

Luckily, my parents know what she's like. They've listened to countless arguments I've had with her. They've even had arguments with her themselves. They know that the worst thing to do in a situation like this is to try and talk to me. They know I'll eventually calm down.

Mum comes over, pats me on the back and takes the plates out of my shaking hands before I drop them, a wedding present from Dad's dead Granny Linda.

There's an awkward silence as we sit at dinner. No one wanting to bring it up. Mum and Dad keep glancing at each other uncertainly every time my fork slips and makes a scraping noise against my plate.

I hear them talk when they're in the living room together and think I'm in bed. Mum says that she hates Stacey and how she treats me and that I deserve more. What sort of life am I going to have being with her? That I should get out now before we have a mortgage. Or get married. Or have a baby. In my mind, I know she's right. But I can't help myself. I'm in love with her. If I could go back in time and tell myself not to go out with her, I would. Save myself the stress that she's caused me over the past two years.

"Let's put the telly on, shall we?"

Mum sings her way to the dinosaur relic that is our kitchen television. My friends sometimes mistake it for the microwave when they're over. It was the first TV set that Dad had ever bought with his own wages. Therefore, in his eyes, it's priceless. Mum gives it the traditional bang with her fist and it jumps into life. It's the news. She sits down just as the first national story is finished. Several minutes later, the beautiful anchor Roberta Mills forces a smile in her lemon suit as she presents the local news.

"Police are still appealing for witnesses of the attack that took place on an 18-year-old school girl in the early hours of yesterday morning. Gemma Norris was walking home from a friend's house when she was attacked and stabbed on David's Street on Promised Hill. Police investigators are-"

"That poor girl," Mum sighs, tears already filling her eyes as she puts down her fork full. "I saw her mother in the supermarket earlier today and she looked awful."

"Well, I'd say you would too if your daughter got stabbed in the stomach," Dad half laughs, picking up his glass of wine. Typical Dad. Trying to make the best of a situation.

"Of course I would," Mum glares at him. "But I wouldn't leave the house. No matter how desperate I was for milk. What that family has gone through is disgusting. I hope he's caught soon."

My phone goes off and breaks the uncomfortable atmosphere.

"Teddy," I laugh, picking up my half-eaten plate and taking it over to the sink. Mum's lips purse when she sees how much I'm leaving, but again, doesn't say anything. Teddy wants me to go out tonight with him and his new flatmates in the town centre. I turn down his offer. After the news I got today, the last thing I want to do is meet his new uni friends and have to tell and re-tell the story of why I'm not at uni too. Besides, I'm still in a bad mood because of Stacey.

I go up to my room and lie on my bed, face buried in the pillow. What a day. I think of texting Stacey to see if she's in a better mood, but decide against it. I don't want to risk a text argument. One of the things I hate doing most. The anger you get as you stab the keys as fast as you can drives me insane. As much as I hate arguing, I'd rather have it out face to face. I'm not one of those keyboard warriors that battle it out behind their phones or computers. They're just cowards. Plus, I'm too stubborn. I've done nothing wrong so why should I go grovelling back?

An hour passes of me flicking through TV channels and checking my Facebook every two minutes before I sit up and start getting ready. Fuck it. I'm going out. Although Stacey doesn't realise it, she's *still* controlling me. She's the reason I'm in a bad mood and I'm not going to give her the satisfaction of knowing that she's the reason I didn't go out and have a good time.

CHAPTER 5:

The glare of the moonlight outside my window leaves an eerie white glow across my room. A part of it comforts me from the demons in the dark. The other part makes me feel like everyone's looking at me. All the pictures in their frames. All the posters on the walls. Their eyes staring at me. Judging me.

I rock back and forth in bed. My toes curled up and my arms wrapped around my legs. I sing the soft tune my sister used to sing to me years ago. I don't know the lyrics. I don't even know what the song is called. Just the tune. Every night while I tried to sleep through the hiccups and sobs brought on by hours of crying.

"It's okay, I'll protect you," I remember her saying. "I won't let anything bad happen. I won't let them hurt you."

The soothing lullaby drowned out the yelling downstairs. The slamming of doors. The screams of pain. The smashing of glass. Somehow it all made it seem alright. Like it was someone else's life. Someone else's family.

As I lay now in my room, I hear the creaks and whispers of the old building. Every noise making me jump. Thrusting my hand under the pillow to reassure myself that it's still there. Calming me like she used to. It will protect me. I can protect myself. I don't need anybody else.

An hour or two later, it starts. I see the shadows under the door. I feel the tension. I hear their sniggers. The rasping and scratching at the door is just the beginning. Slipping on my hoody and sliding the blade inside the front pocket, I start my descent down the drainpipe. I've learned to master scaling the wall successfully without hurting myself or making any noise, apart from the dull thud of my trainers hitting the grass. Skimming under the protection of the thorn bushes, I squirm my way right through my normal escape route until I reach the small hole leading out on to the main road.

Pulling my hood over my head and face, I follow the side of the road where the street lights have been knocked out by local kids. The council hasn't bothered replacing them. The council doesn't bother with much around these parts. Trudging down Jude Street, Browning Avenue, right around the corner to South Evergreen. All the while clinging to the blackness. Facing away from the road when the occasional car passes. I don't have many encounters. Just nurses or doctors on their way back from the big city hospital, or taxis bringing drunken students back from Bar Boss, the biggest night out on a Friday. I hear my footsteps echo off the graffitied brick surrounding me, further influencing my isolation, both on the street and in life.

Slipping into the shadow of complete darkness, I reach the side entrance to Rong Valley Park. My sanctuary. I already start to feel calm as I follow the meandering path towards the sound of the flowing stream. My heart rate drops and my hands loosen on the blade. I bring out my hands and lick my fingers, fresh with blood from all the pressure applied. They've called me a vampire before, so why don't I

27

act like one? The taste of the iron makes me feel sick and I gag slightly as it trickles down my throat. I can't even do that right.

I follow the stream through the forestry and think of them all. So happy with their perfect families and their perfect lives and their perfect friends. It's not fair. I start to get angry again. Reaching the end of the stream where it flows into the mouth of the River Rong, I look across the water towards the lights of the town centre. All those bastards. Complaining about life when they have nothing to complain about. They're just too ignorant and insolent to realise it. They don't know what it's like. They'll never know what it's like. Not unless I show them. I grab the cold black plastic at the base of the knife and charge my way towards the bridge.

As I turn off the bridge and down Benjamin Street, I'm greeted by a dozen alcoholics outside their centre. I've heard about this place. Ben's Palace. It's nothing like a palace. I know I'm at no liberty to be snobbish to other people's living conditions, but I can't help but wrinkle my nose as I walk past the foul smelling middle-aged men.

I look up at the broken stained windows. Their curfew's at 9pm. If they arrive with alcohol in their systems, then they're not allowed in at all. I walk past them all sitting together outside the front door. Resting their heads on each other's shoulders. I step over the one worse off, lying with the bottom half of his body still on the pavement. Vomit from his mouth dropping into a pool beside the grating.

I spit on him. Disgusting. The world would be better off without them. Someone needs to take them off the streets. But not me. Not now.

I've got more important things to worry about.

I follow them from the club. I follow them to the ATM machine. I follow them to the chippy. Watching. Waiting. All the time under cover of darkness. They laugh. They fall. They laugh some more. Idiots. In a way, they're not much better than those alcoholics. The only difference is that they actually *have* a home to go to at the end of the night.

My blood starts to boil. Who will be tonight's victim? The girl with the leopard print dress? The boy in the red checked shirt? The girl with the heels far too high? I wait for my prey to cut themselves loose.

My time comes shortly after four. The seventeenth taxi rang finally comes and four of them jump in. The boy in the red checked shirt bargains with the driver, trying to slip in the back as well. Stupid bastard. Everyone knows the rules. After a few minutes, he gives up and kisses the girl in the backseat goodbye, taps the roof and waves them off. I wait for the brake lights to go out, plunging him into darkness as he meanders his way towards the bridge.

He stumbles down Clement's Lane, the long way around. Probably to avoid the alcoholics on Benjamin Street. He's so blinded with the drink that he doesn't even realise that I'm walking less than twenty steps behind him.

After he walks off the bridge, he turns into Nelson Street. Perfect. We're in complete darkness. Nothing illuminating the street apart from a single yellow pane of light coming from the flats twelve stories up. I see the boy stumble his way up the street and know I have to act soon. He's a few dozen yards away from Upper Dee Street, perfectly lit with a twenty-four-hour shop and several takeaways. I reach inside my pocket and bring out the knife. I grip it tightly, excited to extort its power.

But without warning, my foot slips on a black bin bag. I desperately try to balance and search with my foot for something solid, but fail and hit the ground with a loud crash.

Shit!

Hearing the boy's footsteps stop, I roll over and press my stomach against the wall, holding my breath. Out of the corner of my eyes, I can see the boy has turned half of his body around, facing directly towards me. Subconsciously, I can feel his eyes burning into me.

Several seconds pass before the boy chuckles.

"Stupid cats," he hiccups before turning and continuing his journey.

I exhale a bit too loudly. Thank God for the bin bags or my black hoody would have been obvious against the white concrete of the corner newsagents. I thank God again that the knife was in my hand and not in my pocket. I don't want to end up like my victims. I've done nothing wrong.

He's almost reached the halo of light when I get to my feet. A ray of hope for my still unsuspecting victim. I quicken my pace, twisting the knife in my sweaty palms. He's still stumbling, hiccupping and singing a stupid dance song he must've heard tonight. A few feet from his back, my stalking is interrupted again. I stand on a bit of litter, letting out an almighty crunch which ricochets off the bare walls around us.

He stops abruptly. I must act now.

As he starts to turn his head I grab his neck, thrust it back and plunge my weapon straight into his stomach. I hear him gasp, but he doesn't struggle. He just murmurs. His warm breath in my ear. I feel the hot blood envelope my hand. Beautiful. I pull my blade out and dig it in again, slightly to the right.

I repeat, again and again. Tears in my eyes. Frustration in my throat. I want to scream out. Curse him. Curse his life. I want his soul to escape his body and wrap itself around mine.

"Pick me," I plead. "Pick this body." I want to live with no worries. No bullies or trauma or stress.

I start to weaken. My grasp around his neck loosens. My murderous ways escape from my mouth as I moan. Almost orgasmic. The tension built up inside me has now spilled out onto this unwilling target. Unleashed onto his twitching body. He sinks to his knees as I finally let go. I hear his face splat off the pavement as I stand, arms outstretched, dripping with blood.

A bit messier than expected, but just as satisfying. I listen to the soft droplets of blood hitting the ground from my hands. My hoody. The knife.

Bliss.

CHAPTER 6:

The sound of the water hitting the shower tray wakes me. I stir, grumbling, and push the pillow between my legs. Five more minutes won't hurt. My head's pounding from last night and the taste of alcohol is still fresh in my mouth and lying in my stomach.

The door slams and the lock clicks. My eyes snap open. Stacey must be in one of her moods again. I roll over onto my back and stretch. Half way through yawning, I stop and gaze upwards. I'm greeted by a half-naked poster of Carmen Electra stuck to the ceiling. Don't get me wrong, it's not a bad sight to wake up to. But I'm now aware of my whereabouts.

Sitting up, I look around the room. The guitar in the corner. The dozens of untidy CDs. The clothes thrown all over the floor. On closer inspection, I notice that some are my own from last night.

This isn't Stacey's room. This is Lydia's apartment!

I pull on my trousers and throw on my shirt. As I dart around the room wildly, searching for my shoes, the hum of the water from the bathroom in the next room stops. I spin around and stare at the door. It opens and steam escapes from the room and floods out into the bedroom. Lydia's silhouette comes into focus as she walks in. One towel draped around her chest and another drying her cropped hair. Her pink scaly skin shines in the dull light coming from the balcony window. She walks straight past me as if I were invisible, sits down at the dressing table and lights a cigarette. I leer over her shoulder. Smoking, specifically indoors, one of the many things I can't stand about her. I shift uncomfortably and cough.

"Do you know where my-" I start.

Before I can finish the question, with minimal effort, she kicks out my shoes from under her dressing table, still not looking at me.

"Thanks," I mutter.

My head's throbbing as I sit and tie my laces. The sickness in my stomach now mixed with guilt. My phone vibrates on the floor beside me. I curse, twelve missed calls and eight texts, most of which are from Stacey. I look up to Lydia applying her eyeliner, stretching it right from her eyes to near her ears. Again, another thing I detest about her. I twiddle my thumbs awkwardly.

It's always like this, every time this happens. Drunken texts and expensive taxis. All for one night of lust. One night of passion. One night of meaninglessness. Then in the morning, we're just strangers. Nothing to talk about and she doesn't even look at me. I guess I should count myself lucky this time. Sometimes I don't even make it to the morning. I'm thrown out on the street before I even get a chance to take the condom off.

I stare at Lydia. Applying her makeup, replacing her piercings and spiking her hair. What is it I see in her? Why does she have this control over me that makes me look like such an idiot? What spell does she have on me that makes me forget all about Stacey? And believe me, I don't use the word 'spell' loosely. Loads of people say she's weird and into all that sort of hocus pocus, like some lesbian witch. But no matter how much she hides behind her façade, we both know she's not a lesbian. Not when she rings looking for a ride off me every few weeks. I'm not stupid. I know she's using me. But I can't help it.

Lydia's reflection catches me staring. She fidgets on her seat and pulls her chest towel up a few inches higher.

"I have work soon, you can catch the next bus into town if you leave now."

Liar. I know for a fact she only works nights. But it's an easy escape out of her apartment, so I smile and quietly leave. She barely hears my goodbye, and doesn't give so much as a whisper for her reply.

The dirty doors of the smelly elevator close and I'm lurched downwards, making my stomach feel even worse. My phone vibrates in my pocket. It's Stacey. Again.

'I miss u & I'm sorry, come to my house? Xx'

I look up from my phone and stare at myself in the grimy mirror, fix my untidy hair and straighten up and button my shirt. I sigh, back to normal. Except my eyes. Behind the dark rings and the bright blue iris lies the truth. They give away my secret as the constant blinking tries to hide the guilt and deceit behind them.

The elevator doors slide open as it hits the ground floor. The darkness of the room surrounds me as I trudge down the creepy corridor. The automatic lights switching on seconds after I pass them. As I reach the swivelling doors, I take a look up and down the street. Deserted. Perfect.

I walk down the road, thanking God that I don't know anyone around these parts. My footsteps bounce off the graffiti and the rubbish on the derelict street. I turn up my nose as I walk past a battered dog begging for food. How can Lydia live like this? I suppose she has no choice. After her parents threw her out, she had nowhere to go. Promised Hill is where the council send most people living in poverty.

"James!"

My heart jumps to my throat. Oh, no. Who is that? How am I going to explain this? I turn on my heels, a huge grin on my face. But the road is still as deserted as it was before.

"Up here."

I look up towards the dozens of empty balconies and see Lydia, arms outstretched over the railings. My keys drop onto the pavement a few feet to my right.

"Are you crazy?" I hiss. "Someone could have saw that!"

She shrugs, replaces her toothbrush in her mouth and retreats into her apartment, sliding the glass doors shut behind her. As fast as I can, I scoop up my keys, force them into my pocket and start forward again like nothing happened. I don't meet any more walks of shame on my journey.

Climbing onto the bus, I'm thankful that the majority of seats are empty. I walk past an elderly man and his dog, two 14-year-olds giggling and a young boy who looks to be in a similar situation as myself. As I make my way up the aisle, I see that rough looking kid from the bus yesterday up the back. Only this time he's on his own. He stares at me as I stumble towards him, a look of disgust on his face. His Adidas cap is hiding his greasy hair today, but it doesn't make him look any less of a thug.

I roll my eyes at him and flop down on the seat. Head against the window. I'm still feeling the drains of the hangover. Aware of my phone vibrating in my pocket, I ignore it. Too mentally exhausted to take notice. My conscience is my enemy in situations like these. I imagine a little Jiminy Cricket standing on the chair next to me, frowning with his arms folded, tapping his foot. It's not cheating, I think. Nothing's going to become of us. She's in a relationship with another girl and so am I. Outside the bedroom, we don't speak or associate with each other. I think back on last night to try and remember how I ended up with her, but I drank so much, I don't remember much after the second bar.

My phone vibrates in my pocket again. I clench my teeth against the annoyance, then my eyes widen. My phone! I bring it out and start looking through the texts from last night. Man, I was so drunk. So many of them don't make sense, and the ones that do are embarrassing. Finally, I get to Lydia's. Aha! *She* made the first move. A small victory. Although, I don't really help myself. She texted me at half two in the morning and I texted back less than two minutes later telling her I was in the taxi over now.

Flashbacks start to swim into my mind, but not in order. I remember climbing the stairs towards Lydia's apartment. I remember taking the Aftershock shots at Teddy's flat. I remember hammering on Lydia's door over and over again, just to find that she wasn't home yet. I remember stumbling through the streets trying to wave down a cab. But worst of all, I remember being between Lydia's sheets. Between her legs. Her moaning and groaning as I went to town in my sloppy drunken state.

As the memories come flooding back, my battery dies. I replace it in my pocket and sigh. This time, like many times before, I'm blaming it on the drink. Temporarily making me crazy. The bus turns down Rod Lane and I frown slightly. Why's it not going down the usual route of Nelson Street? I crane my neck and see the flashing blue beacons of the emergency services. What the hell's going on? I let my head fall back on the headrest and exhale slowly as my mind clears.

I get off the bus a stop early and head towards Stacey's house, wiping the guilt and the last of the hangover off on her welcome mat.

CHAPTER 7:

I'm greeted by her dad watching the footie. He calls me into the living room and asks about last night. I tell him it was good, just out with the boys. Down The Old Crown, The Bolt, Spoons. Little does he know I was shagging some lesbian behind his daughter's back, before my friends had even made it to The Mags Pub. Or The Slags Pub, as my friends and I call it. No prizes for guessing why. We start talking about school and all the opportunities I have. The world's my oyster. All that other crap. Upon hearing the creak of the floor boards upstairs, I excuse myself.

As I climb the stairs, my stomach turns again. Sickness this time. I should've stopped off at Myra's chippy around the corner first. A battered sausage would go down a treat right now. I come to the final door at the end of the corridor. The multi-coloured stars, One Direction posters and the pink unicorn with his speech bubble saying 'Stacey's room.' I know she's crying even before I hear her. I knock twice, holding my breath as I let myself in.

She smiles, revealing her pearly white teeth, as she exhales and flops herself down on the bed next to me. She reaches down and pulls the wet crumpled duvet over her modesty, before twisting around and lying on her side, showing just a little bit of nipple. Resting her head on her hand, she stares at me with them eyes. I'm still out of breath and half laugh as she expects me to comment.

"Wow," I say, my heart still racing. "That was amazing."

She purses her lips in approval, swings her legs around the bed and walks towards her en-suite. Despite my satisfaction, I can't help but steal a glimpse at her bare backside. I shuffle down the bed and rest my hands behind my head as my heart rate slows and my breathing returns to normal.

Make-up sex. Always the best. It must be the guilt. We fought for hours, and then she made it up to me. I hear her singing through the crack in the door as she hops into the shower and I can't help but smile. Despite how much hard work she is, it's times like these that make the work worthwhile. When we make up, she's always in such a good mood. We usually rent a movie or order a chinese. She'll actually laugh at my jokes and be all over me. She'll be happy. I love her when she's happy. She's a completely different person.

She comes out of the bathroom. Her pale arms pink with the steam and she smiles over at me. That beautiful smile. I stare at her reflection as she makes her way over to her dressing table. Her eyes luminous in the mirror's lights. Her delicate fingers as she brushes her thick wet hair. Her back, as a single water droplet slides its way down to absorb into her towel. I feel myself starting to get aroused again.

I pull on my boxers as I potter over and wrap my arms around her. She giggles and rests her neck on my chest. We stare at our reflections for a while. I gaze at the dark rings under my eyes, not daring to look into my deceitful pupils in case I give too much away. It takes a few seconds to realise that Stacey is looking straight at my reflection. I panic. She knows! No, she doesn't. She's smiling slightly and her quaint hands are gently stroking my bare arm.

"What?" I laugh.

She beams up at me and pats my arm.

"You better put that smelly shirt back on, I'm sure my granny and granddad wouldn't appreciate you landing downstairs with your chub on," she giggles and pretends to hide her face in shame.

I frown slightly. "Granny and granddad?"

"Yeah, they're coming for dinner tonight."

"Why?"

"For Dad's birthday, I told you last week, remember?"

I stare at the painting of a flower on her wall, straining my brain to remember.

"Erm..."

I feel Stacey clench and move away from me slightly. Shit. Think. Quick.

"I knew you weren't listening, too busy on your bloody phone-"

A light bulb goes off in my head. Of course. Last week. We were in my living room with a blanket and a film. Stacey was on one of her rants about Jessica, her annoying friend. I was half listening to her as I was scrolling through Twitter.

Then Lydia started ringing me. She must've been out with her friends and feeling a bit hetero. My eyes widened as I tried to hide the name on my phone.

"Who was that?" Stacey said, eyes narrowing as she sat up and stopped her story.

"Erm..." I thought. "Not sure, it was a hidden number. Probably one of those annoying call centres."

Stacey stared at me for a while longer. Convinced, she lay back down and continued with her story. Despite Stacey giving up easily, Lydia hadn't. The vibrations were faintly felt or heard through the heavy pillow pressed over the screen. As my eyes didn't move from the TV, I counted five calls and eight text messages. I was so worried about Stacey finding my phone that I hadn't listened to much of what she said.

"Oh yeah, I remember now," I smile. "Sorry, not enough blood in my head to think," I wink at her reflection.

She purses her lips again, this time out of frustration. She starts doing her eyeshadow as I put my legs into my jeans. I pick up my wrinkled shirt, that's when I see the drink stains. With a crumpled nose, I turn to Stacey, the shirt outstretched with my two fingers. Before I have a chance to say anything, she's already giving me a look of disgust.

"What?"

The fire is starting up in her nostrils.

"My shirt-"

"Let me guess. It's a mess. It's disgusting. It smells. You need to go home and change it. Once you get home, something will come up that you can't come for dinner. You're too hungover. You've just been sick. One of the boys has asked you out. You-"

"Stace, calm down."

"-told me you're coming to this dinner and you're not letting me down now! Honestly, James. You're unbelievable."

I sigh and sit on the edge of the bed, waiting for the mood swing to subside. My eyes follow her around the room, gesturing out the window, marching to her wardrobe, throwing crinkled clothes at

41

me. The whole time, I let next to nothing into my head. I've found this is the best thing to do. It saves stressing me out. And to be honest, when I get angry, I just end up making things worse.

When my ears reopen, she's angrily straightening her hair, the wand hissing at me like a snake. As I creep over to the mirror, her reflection glares at me, giving herself even more of a serpent vibe. I bite my tongue, considering what to say.

"Do you want me to smell like sweat and booze when I see your grandparents?"

She stays silent, playing with her hair.

"I can run home, get a shower, clean clothes and drive back over. I'll be less than an hour. It's half five. They won't be here until half six. You know how your granddad drives."

The corners of her mouth twitch, almost breaking a smile.

"I promise," I kiss her on the head, still damp and frizzy. "I'll be back soon."

It looks like Stacey's the one biting her tongue now.

"I'm home," I shout, slamming the door behind me. I'm half way up the stairs before I hear the screaming.

"James? James! Oh, thank God!"

I frown as I slow down. That's Mum. Jumping down the steps three at a time, Mum comes storming out of the living room. My adrenaline's rushing through my veins. Before I get the chance to demand what has happened, I'm absorbed in a pink heart covered dressing gown. She's sobbing uncontrollably.

I tap her on the back empathetically.

"What's wrong, Mum?"

She pulls away. She looks awful.

"You look like you haven't slept in a week," I laugh.

Her eyes widen and suddenly starts slapping me with the phone in her hands.

"Hey, hey, hey, hey."

"Stupid, stupid, stupid boy!" Mum sniffles, before embracing me again.

"Mum, what's happened?"

"Haven't you heard?" Mum leads me by the elbow into the living room, where Dad's sitting in his armchair, head in his hands. As soon as I walk in, he looks up and gives me a nod.

"Where have you been?" Mum sobs, sinking into the sofa.

I gulp. What way can I put this?

"Err... I stayed at Teddy's. Woke up this morning and went over to Stacey's. I'm only home to-"

"You stayed at Ted's? Does he even have a sofa?" Dad chuckles, but stops once Mum glares at him.

"What's wrong? What's happened?" I start to panic. "Is everyone okay?"

"Yes, son. Everyone's fine," Dad says. "It's just-"

"Everyone's fine?" Mum stands abruptly. "Everyone's fine? How would you like to be that boy's dad? I'm sure he isn't fine. His mother isn't fine. His brothers and sisters aren't fine. And that boy sure as hell isn't fine."

Dad stands and tries to console Mum. I'm still left by the door wondering what the hell they're talking about. When Mum's calmed down, she turns to face me, still getting steadied by Dad.

"There's been another attack," she says, wiping her running mascara. "It's all over the news. A boy's been stabbed. A high school student. He was out late last night. The family still have to be informed, so they haven't released the name. Oh, James. We thought it was you. We thought-" she breaks down again.

Dad cradles her head in his arms, comforting her with soft '*sshhhs.*'

"Mum, I didn't know. I'm sorry, I-"

"Why didn't you answer your phone?"

"It's out of battery. I haven't charged it since last night."

"You were out with the lads, how come you needed it?" Dad's starting to get involved. I hate this tension. I hate lying.

"I... I..."

"Was it Stacey again?"

Mum looks up at me, tears still in her eyes, but her face sullener than before.

"Stacey?"

"Yeah. Did she start again?"

I let out a sigh of relief.

"Erm... Yeah, she kept texting."

"For fuck sake," Mum storms out of the room and comes back with a packet of tissues. She *was* texting away at me last night, so technically I'm not lying.

"I should have known. I saw the way she was going on yesterday. I should've guessed that she'd be texting you all night. Ruining your time. As if your day couldn't get any wors-"

"Jenny!" Dad thunders. Mum blushes and starts fidgeting slightly. We both know that when Dad puts his foot down that someone has crossed a line.

"Why? What's wrong?" I look from Mum to Dad, who both shift uncomfortably.

"It's just..." Mum says with a sideways glance to Dad. "... You always tell us how she tortures you when you go out with your friends. Anyway, that doesn't matter. You're home safe and that's the main thing. Too bad the same can't be said about that young boy. It'll be on the news now shortly. Sit down. You might know him."

"Mum, I really have to-"

"James, please. I want to see if I know his parents. I want to let them know how sorry I am. Just please, do this for me."

Sighing, I look at my watch. The news will be on in a few minutes. If it really is as bad as Mum is making it out to be, then it'll be the first news story. I can tell her I don't know him and start to get ready.

I sit down and Mum continues to sob uncontrollably, occasionally looking over at me and whispering things like *'thank God'* and *'that poor family.'*

"An 18-year-old boy was found very badly injured on Nelson Street in the early hours of this morning. Stephen Begley was walking home from the town centre in the early hours of this morning, after enjoying a few drinks with his friends, when he was viciously attacked with a knife several times. Police are appealing for witnesses who may have been in the area between the hours of 3am and 5am this morning-"

"Well, do you know him?" Mum sniffles.

I stare at the TV. At the news reporter. At the school picture above her head. I do know him. He's at my school.

"Yeah," I whisper. "He's in the year below me."

"Oh, no" Mum whimpers. "Where is he from? I must give his mum a call. I might send over a cass-"

But I'm not listening to her. The camera has jumped to a press conference outside the local police station.

"Detective Sargent McNally," Roberta Mills, the same reporter from last night, has her microphone pressed under the policeman's chin. ="Is it true that this brutal attack is very similar to that of Gemma Norris on Wednesday night, Thursday morning? Does that mean that the police force are looking for a repeat offender?"

DS McNally's face drops.

"I'd appreciate it if you didn't put such things into people's heads," McNally spits. "Rong Valley's Police Department are... They are..." he starts tripping over his words. "We are treating both as isolated incidents. In saying that, we're still looking for... For anyone with information on the completely unrelated case to also come forward. The same can be said for our need for witnesses in last night's attack."

"Do you think they're linked?" I ask.

"I doubt it," Dad grunts, putting his feet up on his stool. "These sick bastards usually have a motive. Like women with the same coloured hair or eyes."

"Both victims are students at Rong Valley's High School, does this not make your officers worried that the incidents could be linked?" Roberta isn't giving in easily.

"As said," the policeman repeats through gritted teeth. "The situations are very different. We believe those responsible are two completely different people. I... Umm... I have nothing more to say on the matter of the attacks being linked."

"Gemma went to my school as well?" I stare at the TV with my mouth ajar.

"I didn't know that," Mum sighs. "Maybe they *are* linked."

"Bullshit," Dad snorts. "You heard the officer. He's well ranked. He wouldn't have made it this far without having a good sense of a situation. They're not linked unless the big man says they are," Dad salutes at the TV.

Mum gives a side glance at me and sighs again, dabbing at her eyes.

"I may make a start on dinner-"

Oh, shit! Dinner! I jump from my seat and run up the stairs to the bathroom.

CHAPTER 8:

Look at them. Soaking up the last rays of the summer. Lying on the grass in *my* park. Kissing. Drinking. Playing cards. Bastards. Do they know how much pain they cause me? How it's their fault that I'm the way I am today? How it's their fault that that boy is now critical in hospital? Of course not. All they care about is themselves. Their boyfriends and girlfriends. Their latest iPhones. They'll soon see.

I recognise the boy in the blue t-shirt. I think his name's Derek. He's one of them. One of the bullies. He goes over and puts his arm around a girl. Emily. All tits, no brains. The perfect airhead to be throwing herself over a complete dickhead like Derek. I stare at her tossing her hair back and laughing with her friends, her perfect teeth shining in the sunlight.

I remember them from outside the tennis courts at school. Where the cool kids hung out smoking and skipping class. I was sitting beside the trees, trying to do my homework. My usual spot in the library was taken over by a group of first years stressing over an assignment, so my mood was already dark. Half way through my second to last equation, I felt the clap on my elbow.

"Ahhh," I moaned softly, massaging my arm.

I turned around to see them a few metres away, laughing and pointing. I scowled at them and turned back to my sums. Less than twenty seconds later, a stone landed a few feet in front of me. Mature. I heard the giggles behind me. Once more and I'll move. I grit my teeth, the equations on the sheet jumbling into hieroglyphic nonsense.

The third hit was right to the back of the head. Screwing up my face in pain, my head involuntarily fell forward following the ricochet. They hissed and laughed at me as a trickle of blood slithered its way down my head. I would've turned around. I would've gave them a piece of my mind. I would've showed them they should leave me alone. But my eyes were filling with tears. I couldn't let them see me cry. Imagine. I'd have been the laughing stock of the school. Not that I wasn't anyway. So I picked up my book and trotted off, sulking, to wolf whistles and shouts.

I study Derek's face. The shadow of unshaven hair across his chin. He tries to impress the girls by walking on his hands, before falling over onto his back. A big laugh. Older now, but definitely not wiser. I wonder what they would do if they knew I was watching? If they knew I was only metres from them. If they knew I was staring at them, almost hungrily, whilst rubbing the blade in my pocket.

"Oi, that boy's wanking!"

I jump with fright and turn my head around slowly. Through the bushes, I can see a couple standing hand in hand on the path to my right. The man is pointing right at me. Shit. My hiding place has been found. I stand up slowly, pushing my hood further over my face until half of my vision is blurred by black cotton. I start to back away, feeling and hearing the crunch of twigs and leaves breaking below my trainers. The man lets go of his girlfriend's hand and starts making his way across the grass towards me. I turn and bolt it.

"Come back here you creep!"

49

BRADD CHAMBERS

Thankfully, spending so much time in this park under the cover of darkness, I meander my way through the trees and out onto the street in less than two minutes. Frantically yanking my hoody off, I shove it in my bag. I sit at the bus stop on the other side of the road, panting, on the bench beside an old lady who gives me a look of disgust. If only you knew, love. I see the man emerging from the side path into the park. He looks up and down the busy street, then right at me. My heart starts to pound, but I remain calm, pretending to stare at a bird about two feet to his left. When I manage to steal a glance again, his eyes are busy giving the road a final check, before turning. He returns towards his girlfriend, moving his head from left to right to get a closer glimpse through the trees.

"Someone you runnin' from?"

I turn to the lady with wide eyes.

"No," I say, thinking fast. "I just thought he was someone I knew."

"Who?"

Nosey old bird!

"My brother's mate."

"Looks a bit old to be the same age as your brother."

"He's the oldest, I'm the youngest."

"What you doin' runnin' around with people that age, then?"

"Since when the fuck was it any of your business?"

The old lady scowls, holds the purse in her arms closer to her bosom and turns to face the road, waiting for the number 20 back to her sad old flat. My hand gravitates towards my stomach, but forget the knife's in the bag with my hoody. Probably a good thing. I don't think I'd get away with this stabbing as easily with dozens of witnesses.

Besides, she's not worth it. She's only got a few more years left in her anyway. She might as well spend them being a miserable old bat.

Spitting on the ground, I stand up and trudge my way towards home.

That was a close one.

CHAPTER 9:

I know I'm late as soon as I hang my coat up on Stacey's bannister in the hall. I hear the soft clink of plates in the dining room and wince, knowing they've started without me. Knocking politely before entering the room, the Pattersons great me with their usual '*ahh James*' and '*sit, sit, we're just getting started*.' Well... Most of them anyway. I plonk myself down between Stacey and her grandad, who shakes my hand firmly, a gummy grin on his face.

"James, son. How are you?"

He doesn't let go of my hand until Stacey's mum has dropped a huge stack of carrots on my plate.

"I'm fine. Had a good summer? How was Turkey?"

"Oh, you know," he says, lifting the gravy boat from the middle of the table and shaking so violently he leaves trails of brown juice over the pristine table cloth. Stacey's mum's eyes follow the stains with her lips pursed.

"Same old, same old," he continues. "Lovely place, don't get me wrong. But an absolute nightmare for holiday makers, you know?"

He puts on an awful Eastern European accent. "Oh, Mr Patterson can I interest you in this? Oh, Mr Patterson can I interest you in that? Half the time we've no idea what they're talking about. Don't we not, Marge?"

He lets out a raspy laugh that shows he spent the better parts of his life inhaling cigarette after cigarette, before coughing and spluttering all over his peas and sweet potatoes. When the fit has subsided, he clears his throat and picks up his fork again. My stomach curdles, and I don't think it's the hangover, but I smile and nod along. Stacey told me all about him years ago. Still stuck in his conservative ways of thinking. It's best to just joke along with him than to argue, as Stacey's dad tries to do every time they're around each other.

I drop my arms beneath the table and place my hand delicately on Stacey's thigh, but she pushes it away abruptly. In the middle of one of her grandad's stories, I frown and turn to her, but her eyes are transfixed on the Yorkshire pudding on her plate that she's flattening like a pancake. Like mother like daughter, I think, as I look at Mrs Patterson scooping her peas on to her fork and letting them drop again. Staring at her father-in-law in disgust. Oh how alike they look when they're both angry. Looking at them now, they could be twins.

"...but anyway. James, Stacey was telling us that you have to repeat a year in school?"

I snap back to my senses.

"Er... Yeah. I didn't get a good enough grade in my Maths you see."

"Why the hell would you need to do well in counting stupid numbers if you want to be a historian?"

I blush. Her grandad always loves talking to me about History.

"I - I'm not becoming a historian, I just want to study it."

"Aw no. You've studied History since you started school. You already are a historian boy!"

53

He slaps my back, making the Brussels sprout fall off my fork and roll across the table, coming to a stop beside the wine. I raise my eyebrows in apology to Stacey's mum for the snail trail of gravy, but she's too busy looking at Stacey. Frowning again, I glance between them both. They seem to be having a very hushed conversation.

"What's all this Tom-foolery about? You two women discussing who's washing the dishes and who's scooping out the ice cream?" Stacey's grandad explodes into laughter again, before spluttering into his inevitable coughing.

Stacey's mum smiles. "Oh nothing Pete, continue."

She gives me a sideways glance before tucking into the last of her chicken.

"Well, Beverly, that was delicious," Stacey's grandad burps, before loosening a few buttons on his cords.

Mrs Patterson gives a fake smile before picking up his plate and retreating to the kitchen, no doubt itching to get her cleaning supplies out on the roast dinner graveyard on her good dining cloth.

"Hey, have we heard anything more about the boy who got stabbed last night?"

"I was just watching the news before I came over," I start, ignoring Stacey's not-so-subtle mumble of *'I'm sure that's the reason.'*

"And what of it?" Stacey's grandad burps again.

"They're thinking... Umm... They think the two might be linked."

"What two?"

"The one last night... And... Erm..."

"The girl a few nights ago," Stacey interrupts, glaring her eyes at me.

I nod, hiding my disappointment of her involvement. Once Stacey finds out I know Gemma from school, that will open a whole new can of jealous worms.

"Oh the Norris'," Stacey's granny perks up for what seems like the first time tonight. Slapping her hands to her mouth and dropping the spoon with a huge clunk on Stacey's mum's good china in the process. Thank God she's still in the kitchen.

"Terrible... Terrible," Stacey's grandad splutters into a hanky.

"We would know her granny from the church. Haven't seen or heard from her since."

"But how could they be linked? There's no way."

"High school students," I butt into the couple's conversation. "They both went... Well, go to my school."

"Aww no, that's just a coincidence," Stacey's grandad snorts. "Sure half the bloody town go to Rong Valley High. What are the stupid news readers trying to say now? That you're next?"

We both give an uneasy chuckle, but Stacey bursts into tears and runs out of the room. Seconds later, we hear her bedroom door slamming shut.

"Jesus, it was just a joke," her Grandad sulks, before choking into a tissue again.

CHAPTER 10:

I lie in her bed. Curtain's drawn to block out the sunlight. TV on some stupid chick flick. She says she's away to the off-licence. She'll be five minutes. Just getting a few more beers. I kiss her goodbye and slap her ass on the way out. Now that she's gone, I can check. Grabbing her phone and putting it on private mode, I google my handiwork. I'm proud to see the dozens of articles already posted. My smirk widens when I read the comments section. I love people damning me. Calling me scum. Saying I should go through the same treatment. Be sentenced to death. What way did my parents raise me? But one comment in particular makes me even happier.

'So awful xxxx First Gemma now this xxxx Hope all there families are ok and if the rumours are true and they are linked that no one else will be hurt xxxxoxx'

Oh Lyndzxox23, how right you are. But also, how wrong and naïve you are. Don't worry. Plenty others will be getting hurt. I scroll back up to the video to get a proper look at this policeman. His black hair slicked back and bright eyes reflecting the flashes from the photographers. You can just tell he never had a bad experience in his life. Probably grew up in a massive house with an en-suite, games room and maids to tend to his every need. Now he thinks he's some big shot because he's got a high security job and not living off Daddy's money anymore. I chuckle as he dismisses the reporter's questions about the two attacks being linked. The longer they hold out on seeing what's right in front of them, the longer I can continue. Undetected.

CHAPTER 11:

"Leave it, Roberta!"

Budds slams the latest edition of the Rong Valley's Herald on his desk, startling Roberta slightly.

"We have a reputation to uphold here, you know? Dawson is one of the first to comment on *anything* going on in this town. We can't lose our main source on the inside. If he says they aren't linked – then they aren't. I admire your enthusiasm, but don't go wasting your time and energy on dead end stories. Look at Marc chasing up his story a few months ago. Believing that old lady Hatchet wasn't really dead. Thought he saw her down in London buying a new pair of slippers in Debenhams. Of course she was bloody dead, we covered her funeral for Christ's sake. That stupid misconception played havoc with the Hatchet family and they will no longer speak to us. Don't go burning any more bridges. That's the last I want to hear of it!"

He stands up and pulls a crumpled packet of cigarettes from his back pocket. Sauntering around the room in a desperate attempt to find a lighter, Roberta scoops hers from her bag and hands it over.

"Sorry, sir."

Budds nods, cigarette between his teeth, and makes a grumbling sound as a thanks as he snatches the lighter out of her hands and hobbles out of his office. The only silver lining in the morning meeting was that Roberta had had the sense to close the office door firmly behind her. She was embarrassed enough with her stripping down without the whole floor of the Herald hearing her.

Returning to her desk, she sits down, exhaling dramatically. Picking up her favourite mug, she sees that she's fresh out of coffee. Retreating to the canteen, she finds peace in the solace of the empty room as she waits for the water to boil in the kettle. She had worked her way up the ranks here. First starting as a stupid work experience project at school, but the journalistic bug had bitten her. She asked to help out once a week until she left school. From then, she did everything from distributing papers, helping with television equipment and, of course, making sure everybody in the room had a full coffee mug. She was thankful for her experience, especially the coffee making skills she learned. As a timid 16-year-old, she hadn't touched the stuff. But now, well into her thirties, she couldn't open both eyes without a cup.

As she pours the steaming liquid in to mix with the granules, she continues to think of her progression. When Sophie had went on maternity leave, Roberta had jumped at the chance to take over. After much persuasion, Budds had agreed. Everyone said it was so he wouldn't have to put her on the books, but Roberta believed it was because the editor had had a soft spot for her. One that continued as she got made a permanent member of staff. Getting promotion after promotion, from PR assistant to junior reporter to crime editor and now an anchor, the face of Rong Valley Herald's Television and Online News.

Almost a decade and a half worth of experience of dealing with Budds, she thought she had him wrapped around her little finger. He let her interview the hot new actor that was staying in the local hotel.

He let her sit in on closed courts if the trial had high public interest. He let her do almost anything she wanted. So why wouldn't he let her do this? This was the first time he had proper snapped at her. Sure, he was a grumpy old man now, and didn't as much as offer a please or thanks to any of his staff. But this was different. He had never spoken to Roberta like that before.

Roberta sits back down at her desk, cradling her fresh cup and opening her e-mails. No replies, leads or new information from when she checked just over an hour ago. Not even so much as a charity crying for some free publicity. Roberta nibbles the inside of her lip before looking around at the busy office. Everyone is either on their phones or in hysteric chatter to one another. Too involved in their own stories to worry about hers. Roberta sighs dramatically again.

"Wow this coffee has gone straight through me."

She needn't have even bothered. The only person who heard her was Julie from the neighbouring desk, who held her hand over the phone long enough for a curt 'ssh.'

Entering the ladies, she checks under each cubicle for signs of shoes. Satisfied with her privacy, Roberta opens her handbag and digs out her ancient Blackberry. It had more lipstick stains than a whore house's bathroom and more scratches than the client's backs, but it was her whole life. She couldn't live without it. With a click of her speed dial, her trusty human phonebook answers on the second ring.

"Felix, darling," she coos. "You wouldn't happen to have the number for the principal of Rong Valley High?"

CHAPTER 12:

To say that Detective Inspector Dawson is in a bad mood would be a giant understatement. He's straight off the plane, back from a holiday in Peru that he had had to cut short because of the incompetents of his team. This shit storm will trudge up the other times Rong Valley's Police Department weren't quick off the mark to solve a case. He thanks God that he has Budds regulating the press, to half calm the public down and prevent them from hurling abuse at uniformed officers, and himself of course. No-one loiters in the halls as the bull of a man charges down the corridor towards his office. The sneer prominent on his otherwise soft face.

He reaches the door and slams it shut, the clattering of his window blinds echoing throughout the room. Dawson stands by his window, puts his hands over his face and moans. A soft cough is heard behind him. The DI slides his hands down his face and turns to the intruder. DS McNally is seated in the corner, and stands up, half-hugging the huge incident file in his arms, as Dawson turns towards him.

"This better be good, McNally."

"Yes. Umm... Sorry to bother you sir, but-"

"Spit it out, son."

"-you told me to meet with you as soon as you were back. You wanted to go over the recent atta-"

"I know why you're here, McNally. Now let me hear it."

"Hear it, sir?"

"Hear the progress you've been making."

"Oh. Well – Umm…"

Dawson plonks himself down at his desk, returning his hands to his face. Burying his thumb into his temples in a desperate attempt to ease the oncoming migraine.

"Door to door questioning on Nelson Street has finished, but to no real help. Everyone was either in town on Friday night or in their beds asleep. The CCTV footage is currently being examined, but a lot of the local shops, bookies and takeaways on that street either haven't bothered to get their cameras fixed once they've been smashed in petty theft or the cameras are fake."

"How?"

"I think a lot of the pound shops do them, sir."

"It was a rhetorical question, McNally."

"Oh, sorry sir."

"Anything else?"

McNally stands open mouthed before quickly consulting his file. Rooting through it, he makes noises of uncertainty.

"So, what you're basically saying is that we have no leads?"

McNally bites his lip and looks at his shoes.

"McNally!"

"Umm… Well. No, not yet."

"So what are we doing about it?"

"Well, like I said, we're still combing through footage, but there isn't a lot to help us. Plus, with no street lights the quality wouldn't be gr-"

"What about the boy's movements? Where was he? Who was he with?"

"Yes, well. We have been to speak to him but he doesn't remember a lot, sir. He was quite intoxic-"

"Well then you find out from his friends. Who was he with that night?"

"They got a taxi home from outside Busty's chippy. They thought he would get the next one."

"Well, he must have walked. He was found in Nelson Street. There's two or three ways he could've travelled. Did you collect CCTV and door-to-door around Black Drive? Benjamin Street? Clement's Lane?"

"Umm... Well, we got Black Drive's, yes. I think they're getting reviewed now by-"

"Benjamin Street? Clement's Lane?"

McNally continues to look at his feet. Dawson punches the table, making McNally jump.

"Why did you just assume that he went down Black Drive? It's Monday, McNally. Monday! That's *two* whole days of time we've wasted. This is a rookie mistake. This should all be done by now. We should have the offender behind bars. And what about the girl? Huh? What leads do we have on her attack?"

"Well, there are no CCTV on-"

"No CCTV? Well, we talk to her. Don't we? Find out where she was that *does* have CCTV. Don't let me remind you of the dog's abuse we got in 2007 for failing to recognise that the murderer of Jill Yates was right in front of us the whole bloody time!"

McNally finally looks up to his superior turning towards the window.

"Go out and gather the team. I'm going to do this properly."

"Okay, sir."

The door slides closed and Dawson sighs. Clutching his chest, he reaches for his coffee.

"This job is going to kill me."

He takes a sip, sends a quick text to his wife to let her and his daughter know he landed safe and to enjoy the rest of their holiday. He gazes out of the window for a final time, before composing himself to address the rest of the team. McNally had made a shitty job of this. He would need to step up his game if he wanted to take over from Dawson when he retires. Moving across to the door, he finds it blocked by McNally, once again.

"I thought I told you-"

"You did, sir. But I'm back. I have something to tell you."

Dawson shoulders McNally out of the way and starts down the corridor.

"Yes, well it can wait unti-"

"No, sir. It can't."

Dawson turns to see McNally's face.

"There's been another attack, sir. Only this time, the victim has been found dead."

CHAPTER 13:

Climbing back up the drainpipe isn't as easy as the descent. It took months to remember all the curves in the brickwork and holes in the wall to stick my feet in, in case I lost balance. But I made it. I'm pacing my room now. Too full of adrenaline to sleep or eat or do anything else. It had happened completely by chance, but I almost laughed out loud when I saw him.

Derek. That dick who bullied me.

I was doing my normal rounds of the park when I saw him. What the hell was he doing at that time of night? It was nearly 3am, but yet there he was. The idea just came into my head. Let's show him. Like throwing stones at me, eh? Let's see how funny it is with a blade in your belly. He made his way into the canopy of darkness from the trees and didn't even know I was following suit. Too busy wrapped up in his amazing life to notice me stalking behind him. Getting closer and closer.

I followed him for a few minutes and when he reached the river, he turned left. Up towards the play park and the rows of houses in Pauline's Park facing out on to it. I had to be quick. I didn't take him as a Pauline's Park resident. Those houses were actually quite fancy. Unlike him. He had almost reached the opening where the trees spill out on to the kid's play park. I was about twenty feet behind him when

I realised that we weren't alone. Big Tits Emily was sitting on the swings. When he made his way out into the moonlight, I skirted over to behind a tree. She probably couldn't see me. But just in case. They kissed before he joined her on the swing beside. I gently punched the tree in frustration. This was one of my only shots to get the bastard and I ruined it by dawdling. I rested against the tree and slid down it. What were those two up to at that time of the morning? I wanted to know.

I sat there for about ten minutes, just watching them talk. Finally, they got up and started walking towards me.

Fuck!

I crawled as far as I could away from the path without obstructing my view. Finding a huge tree as my haven, I slipped my head around it, hood up of course. When they reached the trees, they started to climb off track, through the muck and stopped just shy of the tree I was sitting by not thirty seconds before. The closer they got, the more I could hear snippets of their conversation.

"-you can see no one's here. Believe me. We used to hang out here all the time over summer. It's completely deserted."

"I don't know, Derek. I just can't help feeling like someone's watching us."

"Babe, don't be silly. It's just a big bear waiting to tear you to pieces."

He stuck his arms up, pulled a silly face, growled and made a swipe for her. She fake screamed and started to run away, but he grabbed her and wrapped himself around her waist. Her laugh echoed around the park. Luckily my gagging didn't. He kissed the top of her head as she rested it against his chest. His mouth moved down towards hers and they stopped laughing. He moved both hands from her waist. One up her top and the other up her skirt. She no longer hesitated or resisted. Her hands moved from his arm down his trousers.

I couldn't believe what I was seeing. A live porno in the woods. Some people have to pay subscriptions for that. As Derek pushed her against the tree and pulled down her pants, I found myself with my own hands down mine. What? She's hot. Sue me. Derek thrust himself inside her and I wished it was me.

I was done mere seconds before he was. With a short pant, the peep show was over and he re-buttoned his jeans. She giggled and turned herself around to kiss him again. He gave her a short peck before gazing around him again. He looked straight at me and I almost retreated, before remembering it was too dark for him to see. From away over there, if he could even make out the hood of my coat, it probably just looked like a rock.

"Don't worry, mate," I chuckled to myself. "I won't tell anyone about your primary school pecker."

"Bit late now, isn't it?" Derek coughed, reallocating his attention to Emily. "Time for bed, I think. School tomorrow."

"Um... Okay."

Emily pulled her clothes back on and stood up, giving Derek a hug and started walking back towards the swings. As she retreated, I could've swore I saw her silhouette wiping away tears. For a moment, I almost felt sorry for her. Then I remembered I had Derek to myself. I was itching to get at him. In my mind, he was an even bigger prick now than before, but I had to wait until he was a safe distance away from the play park, or risk getting caught. I stalked him for five minutes, glad to see that he was making his way back to the front gate, where he must've came from when I scoped him. I knew he couldn't live in Pauline's Park.

Then I had an idea.

He was sticking directly to the path, so I made my way around the badminton courts and beat him to the stream. It was hard keeping him in sight with the dozens of trees we had to pass, but eventually I saw him shuffling towards me, hands in his pockets and whistling, adding to the effect dramatically. I lay in hiding, hand gripped around my trusty knife and tried to calm my breathing. I was well aware that my past two victims were nowhere near as athletic or physically fit as Derek. I was at a complete disadvantage here. As the sound of the whistling grew nearer, I knew it was now or never. I peeked my head around, expecting to see him a few metres away. But was met with an empty path. I couldn't find him.

Shit! Where did he go?

"What the-"

My head snapped to the right and I saw him level with my hiding spot, staring straight at me with a confused look. Thank God I still had my hood engulfing my face. I pounced from my crouching position and winded him, taking him completely by surprise. He fell on his back and the splat could be heard of his head whacking off the pavement. As I got on top of him, I wrapped both legs around his stomach and waist, my knees pinning his arms by his side to prevent escape. He jolted about and I narrowly missed his shoulder as the knife scraped off the path. His eyes, reflected in the moonlight, widened as he determined the danger of the situation.

"Get the-"

But his last words were lost. I dug the knife straight into his chest. The gurgling sounds and my bloody hand drove me on. Looking back now, it was a bit more brutal than the past two. A crime of passion. I laughed hysterically as I repeated the attack over and over. I genuinely don't know how many blows to the chest and stomach he received. All I know was his body was lifeless when I left him there. I would've spat on him, but I didn't want to contaminate the body with my DNA. Didn't want my ruling of the darkness to be over before it had properly begun.

Looking at my watch, someone will have had to have found him by now. Or maybe he has called an ambulance. Either way, Rong Valley will be thriving with rumours and scared teens. I run across the hall and jerk the old battered computer awake. Looking around to make sure I'm alone, I search Rong Valley's news website. My hand is shaking as I prepare for pleasurable moments of scrolling down and clicking on various stories, tweets, anything to give me the satisfaction. It's like a disease. An addiction. The aftermath is just as pleasurable as the attacks. I love the fact that everyone is looking for answers and I'm the only one that has them. But when the slow as fuck internet finally loads the page, my mouth falls open as I read the headline.

'Local Boy Found Dead In Park.'

What the hell have I done?

CHAPTER 14:

Well, that was the most boring hour of my entire life. Thank God for lunch. I half-jog out of the Geology department at full speed, overtaking everyone packing up their things and am first into the courtyard. I'm met with what seems like hundreds of students swarming from group to group excitedly. Why aren't they going for food? I'm starving. As I start towards the lunch room, sidestepping people running past and nearly banging into a couple of kids from a few years below, I hear snippets of conversation.

"The policeman was huge. He's so scary."

"But why are they here?"

"Haven't you heard? Derek French was found in the park. Dead!"

"What? How?"

"Rumour is he was stabbed to death. They think it's the same guy who got Gemma and Stephen last week."

"Do you think he went too far this time?"

"I don't know. Maybe. Only one way to find out."

They turn and see me staring at them and shut up. I smile politely and continue on my journey. Holy shit. This is insane. But why are there police everywhere? Are the incidents linked? Could the killer be preying on us? I make a beeline for Deans' office. I want some answers.

The phone in Deans' reception is ringing off the hook. His receptionist is standing at the door into the corridor, reassuring students that everything is going to be alright. Trying to keep them as far from Deans' door as possible, as the stampede of people try to break through. She sees me and sighs. She makes a gap between her arm and the door frame to let me slip past. I ignore the rebellious shouts of '*why is he allowed in?*' and '*what's he doing?*' Opening the door to a dark office, I flick the switch and see Deans hunched over his desk. He doesn't so much as look up when I close the door and take a seat in front of him.

"What a mess, James," his voice is muffled between his upper body and the desk.

"What's going on?"

"Well, I'm sure you've already heard-"

"Yeah, but why students? Do the police think they're linked?"

"I don't know, James. I wish I did. I'd love to know who is doing this to my kids and give them a piece of my mind." Deans finally looks up and reaches for his coffee mug.

"But yes, now they think they are linked. But *don't* repeat that. They don't want the journalists to have a field day, which they inevitably will. All three victims went to this school after all. We'll be getting swamped in no time. I already had a call from Roberta Mills this morning, before I'd even heard about the third attack. They must already be one step ahead. The police seem to believe that a student is responsible. They're beginning questioning this afternoon."

I stare at him, mouth open, shocked.

"What? A student? How? No one here-"

"That's what I keep telling them, but they seem set that the guilty party goes to this school. You'll be one of the first to be questioned. They seem-"

"What? Why? What have I done?"

"Well, not you personally, James. But they're starting with the highest year and making their way down. They believe that if they can't find the attacker, now promoted to killer, that someone will know something. I keep telling them to quit while they're ahead. There's no way my students would be capable of something like this. Sure, there are some kids who could put up a fight outside clubs, steal a few packets of sweets from the local shop. But stabbing and killing someone? I just don't understand it, James."

"Me neither, I was out the town drinking on Friday night when that Stephen boy was attacked. It could've been-"

"Save it for the police, mate," Deans takes another slurp of his coffee and grimaces slightly.

CHAPTER 15:

I run back into my room and crash under the covers. My back to the door, staring at the grubby white wall.

Shit!

I'm starting to hyperventilate. I'm a fucking killer. A fucking murderer. What the fuck have I done? After a few minutes, I calm myself down from having a full-blown panic attack, sit up and put my head in my hands. This is it. It's gone too far. I need to stop. I thought it was a bit of fun, but now? Oh my God. I killed someone! Don't get me wrong, the bastard deserved it, but I shouldn't have been so careless. It's okay. No one knew where I was last night. No one saw me on my journey to the park. No one would know my vengeance towards Derek... Hopefully not, anyway.

I slap myself in the face. I don't know why. It seems to work in movies. I need to stop it. If anything goes wrong, I need to be confident. Sure, Derek bullied me. But he also bullied everyone else. He was a dick. There will be dozens of people who would wish him dead. And after all, like I said, it happened completely by chance. I didn't set out to attack him. I didn't even know he was going to be there. As far as the police are concerned, I was in bed sleeping the whole night. I look at my reflection in the cracked wardrobe mirror.

"Derek French?" I put on my shocked face. "Why does that name ring a bell? He's dead? Wow. That's awful."

My awed mouth turns into a sly grin. I've got this. Regardless, this is murder. Not a measly GBH case. Best to lie low for a while...

CHAPTER 16:

Rong Valley High's front gate is crowded with police cars, journalists and angry parents wanting their sons and daughters to come home safe with them. Roberta sits in her Ford Focus, knowing full well from experience that standing out in the midst of the madness is no good. Better to step back and watch the action unfold. It's a good thing that Mr Deans wouldn't make a statement regarding the last two attacks on the phone with her earlier. If Budds knew that she had went behind his back for no good reason he would've had her job. But he wasn't shouting at her now. Well... He was. But shouting at her to get to the school as quickly as possible. Nothing like a good murder to put the fire under his ass.

After lunch, most of the parents have finished fighting with the policemen and return home, reassured that their babies are perfectly safe within school grounds. Oblivious to the fact that rumour is that the killer could be sharing a classroom with their little cherubs. When policemen continue to turn down interviews and are sick to death of repeating the same old 'a *statement will be given*' and '*no one is available for comment at this moment*,' the journalists retreat to their cars. A handful seem to return to their editors, or scurry off to their next story. But a large quantity, Roberta included, wait patiently across the road. School Lane is tight enough come home time, never mind with the added congestion of police cars and the vehicles belonging to the journalists and news crews. Roberta lets her window down just enough to eavesdrop on Claire, the bitch from the national press who always battles for her limelight, speaking to camera with a panoramic view of the school grounds. But she has nothing of worth. Nothing Roberta already knows. No one does. All they know is that a body was found in the park and they were a student here.

Police are tight-lipped about everything, more than usual. But then why shouldn't they be? A small town like this never ends up on national news for murder. A small town like this never ends up on national news for anything. Roberta has a feeling that this media frenzy is only going to get worse. This will be like the murder of Jill Yates all over again. She looks at the digital clock on her dashboard. Only another half hour until school is let out. Then maybe with the kids away home, they will get some answers.

It's shortly after four o'clock when Detective Inspector Dawson stands in front of the school gates, dozens of microphones shoved under his chin. Roberta easing hers just millimetres from his face. Always having to be in the lead.

"An 18-year-old boy was found dead in Rong Valley Park this morning. His family have been informed so we can confirm the identity of the boy as Derek French, a student here at Rong Valley High. Derek was a popular member of the class amongst his peers and the teachers. He will be sadly missed.

"At this moment, we *are* treating the death as suspicious. Therefore, we are opening a murder investigation. We, in the police force, are treating this crime and the two attacks on fellow students,

Gemma Norris on Thursday morning and Stephen Begley on Saturday morning, as linked. We believe the person or persons guilty of the offences are still at large. We urge caution amongst everyone, not just students at this school.

"Investigations are currently being run to link the three attacks and bring down our perpetrator. Until we can fully understand the reasoning behind these attacks, I can guarantee that more uniforms will be on the streets. We recommend a curfew in isolated areas, such as the parks, and perhaps on quiet streets also. Anyone acting or looking suspicious should not be approached, but should be reported to the police, or alternatively for those wishing to remain anonymous, by calling Crimestoppers. Look after yourselves."

"What was the cause of Derek French's death?" Roberta almost grazes the DI's chin with the mic.

"The body is still being examined as we speak. A statement will be released to press when findings are concluded. That is all."

Dawson turns his head from the lenses of the cameras and the eagle eyes of the journalists and retreats back across the school's carpark. Away from the uproar of questions that will be left unanswered. For now anyway.

CHAPTER 17:

I wait outside Deans' office patiently. I don't know why I'm so nervous. I have nothing to hide. But it's been a mad few days. Reporters trying to hound us on our way through the school gates. Asking us if we were scared. If we knew Derek. If we know who did it. People getting taken out of class. Some returning moments later. Some taking a while longer, but looking shaken and avoiding eye contact. Some not even returning at all. All of them saying the same thing.

"We're not allowed to discuss anything. You'll see when you get called."

I don't like this new life. Your first week back at school after the summer is always awful. Especially for me, as I'm not even supposed to be here. But this is making it so much worse. I guess I shot myself in the foot a bit when I told my Geology and Chemistry teachers that I didn't have any intention on doing well in their classes. I was just there to stay in school. Both scorned at me and walked away. Helping the students in the year below who sniggered at me. Pointed and whispered about me. It's like I'm some sort of alien they've never seen before. In those classes, I stared at the door. Half waiting and half wanting to be called to get me out of those boring as shit lectures. I can't believe Deans put me in those classes. What was he thinking? But of course, knowing my luck, I was called during Maths. The one subject

I have to actually pay attention in to get myself out of here and join my friends at uni.

I stare at the gold plaque on Deans' door and think about how he's tried to help. Everyone gives him a lot of stick and says he doesn't do much, but I'm genuinely happy that he tried to sort me out this year. We've always been good friends, ever since my first week here. Typical me, in the principal's office within my first week. To this day, I still don't understand why I was in there. All I did was tell Mrs Reilly, the Religious Studies teacher, that her subject was a pile of crap and that I would rather do extra classes which would help me in the long run, instead of spending an hour a week learning about '*The Almighty God*,' who, in my opinion, never paid much attention to me.

I was waiting for Deans from half ten that first Thursday morning. The receptionist didn't even look up from her computer when I walked in and asked for him. She merely pointed towards his office and took a sip from her steaming coffee. Very polite. I knocked and peaked through the door to an empty dark office.

"Sir?" I switched on the light and my mouth opened in awe.

It was nothing like my old principal's office, or any other principal's office you could imagine. The walls weren't filled with boring old pictures of boring old past principals doing their boring old jobs. They were plastered in framed pictures of a middle-aged man shaking hands with members of old rock bands my dad used to listen to. ACDC, Thin Lizzy, you name it. Several tables around the room held stereos and sweet-smelling candles that made you feel high, not dying plants or rows of dusty books. His desk was bare and shiny. It looked like it had never been worked on. The only thing that convinced me that it wasn't brand new was the single ring mark where he clearly left his mug of coffee on a daily basis. I sat down on the opposite side of the furnished desk and gazed around at the office, which looked more like a teenager's bedroom.

Deans showed up shortly after 11. As soon as he stumbled in the door, I saw he was the one in the framed photos, and I knew he wasn't your average principal. What little hair he had on his balding head was untidy and poorly kept. His suit was quite scruffy and looked like it hadn't been ironed. He wore a Mickey Mouse comic book tie and his red socks were clear under the trousers, which were a few inches too short for him. His skin was dull and faded, except for his huge rosy cheeks, and his eyes looked like they had never stopped sparkling. He shook my hand warmly and asked what the problem was. I shifted uncomfortably on the chair and looked at my feet. Seeing how nice he was made it worse. He must not have known I was there for punishment. Reluctantly, I started telling my story.

When I had finished, I looked up at him. His expression was still the same, his half smile didn't fade from his face. He tutted and sat down at his desk.

"Oh, James," he said. "James, James, James, James, James."

He leaned back in his chair and gazed out of the window behind him, onto the far-off street. I looked about me, considering whether I should answer him or not. Several moments passed. I almost felt like he had forgotten about me, but then he jumped up from his seat and sauntered over to the office door. He spun around and looked at me as he opened it behind him.

"Mrs Reilly can be a right crying bitch when she wants to be," he smiled at me. "But Religious Studies is compulsory in all schools until you sit your GCSEs. My advice? Just don't listen to her and keep yourself occupied. Students say she gets into the bible like she was part of it, and no doubt she's that old she could well have been. Just sit at the back and do homework or something. Think of it as a free period, there's no exam after all. Have a nice day, James."

I remember I stared at him dumbfounded, my mouth open slightly. I blinked a few times before standing up and crossing the room.

"Erm... Okay... Thanks, Mr Deans."

"James, please," Deans' smile erupted over his tired looking face. "Call me Deans."

Since then, we got the chance to catch up almost every week. Mrs Reilly wasn't too happy with Deans' advice on not listening to her lectures. Some weeks, I would do my homework or revise. Keeping myself to myself and didn't make a fuss. But most of the time I was too lazy and brought in comics or plugged in my earphones.

But no matter what, she would somehow find a reason to send me to Deans. Her reason? For 'disrupting the class,' even if I didn't open my mouth. She just did it to spite me, to be honest. I never mentioned that her vendetta against me worked in my favour, and that Deans and I got on really well and spent the times in his office getting to know each other. As my GCSEs loomed closer, I was half convinced to just walk past her classroom towards Deans' office. But if I did that, I would give her the satisfaction of complaining that I wasn't showing up. So every week, at the start of Religious Studies, I walked in with a huge smile on my face, acting as casual as possible to wind her up.

After my GCSEs, I still went to visit Deans. We no longer had Religious Studies, but I had free periods and I went for a chat. He had the most outrageously funny stories. He was somewhat of an idol. Stuck in this fifty-something-year-old's body, but didn't want to grow up. He still did all the things he wanted to. He didn't let his age or job stop him. He talked about how he went to a gig and got so drunk he was kicked out of the venue. How he got caught speeding to impress his friends. How he lusted over this girl since he was my age. Of course, I shared my problems too. Not just normal shit you share with your principal like school and bullies, but girl and family problems. What I wanted to do when I grew up. What I was doing at the weekend. We were like best friends. My own mates teased him and thought he was weird because of his funny walk and his messy clothes, but I always defended him.

To be honest, he's the only reason I did English for A Level. I told everyone it goes well with History and will look good on my CV, blah-blah-blah. But I did it because he taught the subject. Our friendship in the classroom grew. The rest of the class would leave for lunch or to go to their next class whilst we'd still be discussing the poem, story, play or nothing in particular. He's a fascinating man, and now I'll have the chance to socialize with him again for a further year.

"James Kingston?"

I look up and see the bald head of DI Dawson peering around from the door frame of Deans' office. He's been here all week patrolling the halls at lunch time. Telling us that if we have seen or do see anything suspicious or odd to contact him immediately. I smile and stand up, swinging my bag around my shoulder.

"It's okay. You can leave that here."

I drop it and kick it beneath the empty seat, no doubt being replaced with the next kid to be summoned. My nerves still don't go away as I sit in the same seat I sit in every week. Right in front of the principal's desk. Only this time, I'm not greeted by the smiling face of Deans in his big leather chair. DI Dawson sits with his huge elbows on the desk, his fingers interlocked and resting on a bulging folder. As I glance down, I see my school picture from last year gazing from the page up the DI's nostrils. All the details of my grades, behaviour and after school activities spilled out in front of him like some weird crime case study. Deans is perched at the side of the room in an office chair he must've taken from one of the IT suites. He looks odd cowering in the corner.

"Alright, James," the DI snorts. "I understand you've been kept back a year, correct?"

I explain the story that I'm sick of telling everyone.

"Fine, fine. Well, this will probably be short enough as I doubt you've had much contact with this year group, am I correct?"

"No, basically not at all. Well, my cousin Becky is in it, but I barely see her. Only family occasions and the odd Christmas. I'd say hello to her in the corridor, but that's about it."

I pinch my leg discreetly. I'm blabbing, but there's no way I'm mentioning that I do know someone in the year below. Very well. Lydia. The DI writes down my answer regardless and I cringe. Hopefully I haven't got Becky in trouble. It's always one of those things. Although you know you've done nothing wrong, you still tighten up when walking past or talking to the police.

"Okay. Well, James, I'm guessing because you're basically the new kid at school that you don't know an awful lot. So unless there's something you'd like to tell me?"

The DI looks me straight in the eye, his pen hovering over his page.

"Erm... No?"

The DI smiles and nods.

"Okay, we'll just move on to eliminating you from our enquiries. Where were you last Wednesday night?"

"I was at home. I was in here with Dea... Mr Deans all day, trying to sort things out with universities. Then I came home and sat with my mum and dad and went to bed around 11."

"And they can vouch for you?"

"I'm sure they can."

The DI is silent for a moment as he scribbles my alibi.

"Okay. What about Friday night?"

I freeze. Shit!

"Um..."

The DI looks up and purses his lips. I stammer for another few seconds before he puts the pen down and folds his arms.

"Is there a problem, James?

"No... No. Was just trying to collect my days. I spent all week in this office, it kind of all blurred into one."

I glance at Deans who smiles sympathetically back at me.

"I went home from school and had dinner with my folks. Sat in my room for a few hours and then went out with my best mate."

"Who is?"

"Teddy."

"Teddy Brown, sir" Deans interjects. "He used to go here too. Just about twenty minutes up the road at Byron University. Am I right, James?"

"Yeah, studies Sociology."

I pinch my leg again. Why did he need to know that? The DI gazes at me a minute longer, nodding his head and chewing his lip. Finally, he starts writing down this new information.

"I presume his given name isn't Teddy?"

"No, sir. Ted Brown."

"Short for Theodore?"

"No," I half-laugh. "He hates that."

"My grandad was called Theodore."

The DI looks up again and frowns at me

"Oh…" I look down at my feet, shifting them uncomfortably.

"Anyway, so you were with him all night?"

Fuck!

"Yes."

"Where did you go?"

"Into town. Spoons. The Stag and Deer. Those sort of places."

"James, I'll need a full timeline of your whereabouts to be able to remove you from our investigations. For all I know, you could've been in the same pubs as Stephen."

"Right, right, of course," I fumble with my tie. "Well, to be honest, I was quite drunk. I had found out that day that I had to come back here for another year, so I was in quite a bad mood, so wanted to drown my sorrows a bit. We started off at Teddy's flat-"

"Which is where?"

"Off the Bridge Road. The student halls. I can't remember the name exactly. Apollo Halls or something like that?"

The DI nods for me to continue.

"Then we went to The Old Crown for a few shots. Cheap enough there you kn-"

"We're going to need times here, James."

"Oh. Sorry. Well, I think we left the flat about half past ten. We arrived at-"

"Bit early to be going out on a Friday night, don't you think? Whenever my daughter has her friends around, they don't leave til gone midnight."

"Yeah, well… The Old Crown closes quite early so we wanted to get a few drinks there beforehand."

"You said something about shots?"

I blush.

"Yeah. Teddy and I always get a few shots of Sambuca in there."

The DI wrinkles his nose as he's writing, almost making the situation laughable.

"So we left there about… 11? Quarter past? Made it to The Bolt and stayed there for about an hour and a half. Made it to Spoons about… Say one? Stayed there for about another hour and a half."

Shit! Now what do I say? I get the flashback of standing at the bar and checking my phone. Seeing Lydia's text, slipping out the back door of Spoons and thumbing down a taxi. I can't tell them where I've been. Deans knows I'm in a relationship and Lydia wouldn't be too happy either. And what if they want to talk to her? Confirm my alibi?

"Then about half two we went for last rounds at The Slag – I mean, *Mag's* Pub. Then at about four o'clock we stumbled home."

"You mentioned The Stag and Deer?"

"Did I? Must've been another night. We usually go there."

"What about Bar Boss?"

"What about it?"

"Isn't that the best place to go on a Friday night?"

"Yeah, well I've been there a few times, but not that night."

"Are you sure?"

"Yes."

The DI looks at me a moment longer before closing his notebook.

"We'll be checking CCTV in the pubs you say you've been. Some of them match up with those Stephen and his friends say they've visited. You have no problem with that, do you?"

"No, of course not," I strain a smile.

"Good. So you think you got home about, what? Four thirty? Quarter to five?"

"Must be. Like I said, I don't really remember."

"Your mum and dad would know, would they not?"

Shit!

"Erm... Yeah. No actually, I slept over at Teddy's that night."

"Okay. Taxi?"

"I think so. Like I said... Don't really remember," I laugh, but am uneasy at his gazing stare.

"And Sunday night?"

"I was in my house all night. Didn't leave until 8am Monday morning."

"Fine. If any other information comes creeping back into your inebriated brain, you know where to find me?"

"Of course, sir. Thanks."

I stand and slide towards the door, feeling his eyes burning through the back of my head all the while.

"Goodbye, James," Deans waves me out.

As I leave his office, I'm greeted by that scummy kid who I saw on the bus drawing all over my school bag.

"Oi!"

He looks up and sniggers, dropping my bag to the floor.

"Johnny Kitson?"

He walks past me into the office and we glare into each other's eyes until DI Dawson shuts the door in my face. I pick up my bag and exhale infuriated. He had drawn cocks and wrote every curse word under the sun all over my bag. I hate that kid. Maybe an hour with DI Dawson will knock some sense into him. Starting down the corridor, my journey is interrupted when the lunch bell rings. Well, that's one lesson I'll have missed. Sighing, I make my way straight to the canteen with the meeting still on my mind. That was a close one. But I can guess that this won't be the last I'll see of DI Dawson.

CHAPTER 18:

It's been a long week. Jumping every time the phone rings or there's a knock on the door. Expecting the police to grab me and handcuff me to the ground every time I see flashing blue beacons. Turning around defensively every time I hear footsteps or see a silhouette behind me. And the paranoia! I never thought I'd be reacting like this. I thought I was stronger. A lot of the time I brush it off and laugh at myself. If I don't get my act together, I'm going to give off suspicion. Give the game away. I think it's made worse with the stupid curfews. I'm longing the safe haven of the trees in my park. But if someone sees me anywhere near there, I'll be presented with questions I don't have the answers to. But I need to get back there. Calm myself down by the river. Get away from society and have my own time again.

The story was, naturally, headline news. Not just here, but many of the national press were picking it up. But over the past few days it's dropped from first to second in the segment. From second to third, and so on. Now it has vanished from the main storylines completely. Nothing but a tiny scroll box at the bottom of the TV. Surely that's hardly enough interest to pay the excessive number of officers currently patrolling the streets? It'll calm down. I just need to hold out a while longer.

The scratches and taunts coming from my bedroom door make the situation worse. Do they know? The haunted features of the posters on the walls plague at me. I've cried myself to sleep one or two nights. I talk to her on nights like that. Asking her for help. She said she would protect me, but she can't protect me from them.

CHAPTER 19:

Roberta sits patiently in the hall. From where she's sitting, she can look into Room 15A perfectly. However, she only hears snatches of conversation. She smiles at the passing nurses and patients and checks the time *again*. Visiting hours had finished five minutes ago. Why were the Begley family still surrounding Stephen's bed? Showing up at a patient's bedside is the ultimate door-stepping. They can't reject entry, but can still refuse to talk to her. Or even worse, get Roberta escorted out. Not to mention the abuse the Herald would get if word got out on social media. She's risking a lot to speak to Stephen. Luckily, she has a charming manner and this isn't her first time out in the trenches.

When the family finally leave, Roberta waits a few minutes before standing up, fixing her skirt and looking up to come face to face with Stephen himself. She gives him a huge smile, which he returns half-heartedly and waddles his way to the toilets.

"Shit," Roberta exhales. Now he's seen her, although he didn't know who she was, she can't use the element of first impressions. She retreats down the hall and waits for him to return to his room. Moments later, she peers around the door of the room. His roommates are three older men. The man on her right clucks with his false teeth, failing to eat a yoghurt. She makes a pantomime of looking at the name on the board above his bed regardless. After repeating the charade with the other two, she comes to rest in front of Stephen's bed. Satisfied that he has seen her checking his board, she smiles at the boy again.

"Hi, Stephen. I'm-"

"I asked for red, but they only had green. Sorry, babe."

Roberta's eyes widen as a young brunette girl comes marching in and slops a tub of jelly down on the hospital table hovering over Stephen's knees. She recognises her as the girl with his family.

"It all tastes the same anyways."

She flumps herself down on the green armchair before reaching for a copy of some gossip magazine. Their eyes meet and she retreats her hand.

"Umm... Can I help you?"

"Yes. You must be Stephen's girlfriend?"

"Yeah. You are?"

Roberta bites her tongue at the girl's rudeness.

"I actually haven't formally introduced myself to Stephen yet," she extends her hand and Stephen shakes it timidly.

"My name's Roberta Mills. I'm-"

"You're off the telly," the girl splutters.

Interrupted. Again.

"Yes, dear. I am. I wanted t-"

"We're not speaking to the press."

Why don't you let your boyfriend speak for himself? Roberta feels like asking her.

"Didn't you hear the family wants respect at this time without the likes of you-"

"Yes, I am fully aware. I *did* report on the matter," Roberta gives the girl her fakest smile. "Now, if I could get a chance to speak, I can tell you why I'm here."

"Don't tell her anything, Steve."

"Yeah, Ali, thanks. But I'd like to hear what she has to say."

The girl, Ali, looks at Stephen shocked, before leaning back in her chair and crossing her arms. Roberta almost feels smug as she watches her.

"Yes, well. Hi, Stephen. As you probably already know, I'm Roberta Mills from Rong Valley's Herald, TV and Online news. I'm awfully sorry to have to have met you in such dire circumstances."

Roberta ignores the snort from Ali.

"But, as we both know, your attacker is still at large. Not only that, but the police have finally made the connection between the attacks on Gemma Norris and yourself, as well as the murder of Derek French. I know this is horrible to say, but from a journalistic point of view, the story needs some personality to it. Our readers and viewers are sick of seeing DI Dawson's bald head."

She waits for a hearty laugh. None come.

"If I can get an exclusive from you," she continues. "We can get the story back in the news. Get a bit of empathy going around the community. A face to the name, so to speak."

Roberta places her hand delicately on Stephen's leg, to the horror of Ali.

"I don't know," Stephen bites his lip. "What has Gemma said about it?"

Roberta's eyes widen, but her smile doesn't fade.

"Erm. Well... We've been struggling to contact her, sweetheart."

"And why's that?"

"Well, she's been discharged from hospital and home safe and sound. We've tried to get in touch with her, but her parents won't let us near her."

"So, let me get this straight. You see Stephen as an easy target because you can just flounce in here whenever you want?"

Roberta, getting really fed up with these interruptions, has to bite her tongue to stop herself from telling Ali that visiting hours have been over for a while.

"No, Ali. I don't. But I *do* know that he's an 18-year-old man who can make his own decis-"

"Why don't you go ambush Gemma seeing as she's the ideal victim? Blonde hair, blue eyes. Perfect front page spread."

Both Roberta and Stephen look at Ali for a moment.

"What?" she shrugs her shoulders at Stephen. "Criminology class."

"Look, Ali. I understand where you're coming from. I know between Gemma and Stephen that she has gotten the most publicity and empathy. But you have to remember that she was the first attack, she's a girl and someone was killed directly after Stephen. We believe that the same bastard who did this to Stephen has killed Derek. An innocent life has been taken. You should feel grateful that it's not Stephen lying in the coffin right now. We need to find out who it is that's doing this."

She turns her attention back to Stephen now.

"Stephen, your story is important. Just as important as Gemma's. We need to keep people on the lookout. We've got very little from the police, so your words of truth are priceless. What do you think?"

Stephen continues to bite his lip whilst giving a side glace at Ali, who looks away, finally admitting defeat.

"Erm… What do I have to do?"

Phew, Roberta thinks.

"A picture of you here would be ideal. I'd also need other pictures of you enjoying life. Playing football. Socialising. Anything like that is golden. Then, a timeline of your events that night. Who you came into contact with. And last but not least, the incident. I know it's been traumatic. You probably have only told the police, the doctors and perhaps even some of your family the experience you went through that night. But the colour of this article is going to come from your pain. Your anger at what this man has done to you. Leaving you in a hospital bed."

Ali's openly crying now, even Stephen's wiping away a tear.

"Okay. I'll do it. But how much are you paying me?"

CHAPTER 20:

The Herald's headline almost protrudes out of the front page on DI Dawson's desk as he sits in his comfortable chair.

'*I Never Saw His Face.*'

Dawson sighs as he stares at the picture of Stephen Begley in hospital. His girlfriend at his bedside. Holding his hand and looking almost as solemn as Stephen, minus the bruising and cuts to his face.

'*Full story, pages 4 & 5.*'

"Sir?" Dawson's page turning is interrupted by McNally hovering at the door.

"Yes?"

"I take it that you *have* seen this morning's Herald, then?"

"Yes, of course, McNally. I was the one who gave Budds the go ahead."

"Sir?"

"He was right. Raising public awareness when the investigation is running dry *is* the best thing to do. Hopefully people will read the personal account and it will refresh their memory. I want a few more uniforms manning the phones, understand?"

"Of course, sir. But what about the other press that are ringing?"

"Tell them the same thing we've continued to tell them all week. For now, Budds is the first to get any new material. I owe him as much."

McNally nods and exits. Dawson clears his throat, picks up his coffee and gets to work on the double page spread on Stephen Begley. Mills sure did go out of her way on this one. He glances around the text at the photos to draw people in. Stephen at the local youth club helping kids. Smiling for his school photo. Painting the boy in a perfect light to attract empathy. Dawson is a quarter of the way through the second page when he is, again, interrupted by McNally.

"McNally, this better be-"

"It is, sir, I promise. A woman has phoned in. The boy was sighted that night, just outside her flat. And so was the attacker."

Ingrid Bloom sits on her lumpy sofa. Arms folded and legs crossed towards the wall, away from the interlopers she so gracelessly showed in. Her hooked nose just about holds up her thick glasses and her lips are so pursed it looks like it's visibly hurting her teeth to keep them like that. Dawson coughs awkwardly before repeating himself.

"Mrs Bloom, if you could, did you see the attack on Stephen Begley on Saturday September 10th?"

Ingrid's eyes glance at Dawson's large face, before turning them back to her fireplace. She tuts and shakes her foot slightly. But still looks like she isn't going to utter a word.

"Mrs Bloom. Excuse me for being rude, but it was *you* who contacted us saying that you had information regarding the case. Is that true?"

Still no response. McNally and Dawson glare at each other and stand up, making their way to the wooden front door to their left.

"We can see you're busy. And so are we. We'll leave you in peace. If you decide you want to talk to us, then you know where to ca-"

"Wait!"

They turn and Ingrid is pointing at them. She gasps and resumes her original position. The pair exchange glances again before returning to their seats.

"Mrs Bloom. Have you something to say? Wasting police time is a serious offence. You could be imprisoned or a heavy fine set upon yourse-"

"Okay, okay. I'll talk," Ingrid overdramatically spreads her arms and legs, before slapping her hand to her head. "But only because you made me."

"Mrs Bloom, we aren't making you do-"

"I'm not married."

There's an awkward silence.

"I'm sorry?"

"It's okay. You didn't know."

"No, Mrs… Miss Bloom. I mean I'm sorry as in - can you explain yourself?"

"I was married. A long time ago."

Ingrid looks like she's going to burst into tears.

"Okay. So, what have you to say about the recent att-"

"I shouldn't even be talking to people like you. You made it worse. You took him away from me."

Dawson is growing impatient.

"I'm sorry, Miss Bloom."

"It's Mrs Bloom."

Dawson grips the pen in his hand so tight he thinks it may shatter.

"Okay, we're going to go. If anything else com-"

"No, no, no. Sit down, sit down. I'll make a cuppa."

Ingrid is on her feet and pushes Dawson back onto the sofa with surprising force. She moves around the sofa and into her conjoined kitchen. Muttering to herself, she starts fussing with the mugs.

"Where the hell did you find this one, McNally?" the DI hisses in a whisper.

"She phoned in. Said she saw the whole attack."

"She's an unreliable witness, don't you think? Seems a bit bat-shit crazy. Maybe she just heard the attack went on in her street and wanted a bit of-"

"Here we go," Ingrid sings, as she hands the mugs to the officers. They thank her, take a sip and nearly spit it out. It's freezing. She clearly forgot to boil the kettle.

"Lovely, nice and milky," McNally smiles before placing the cup on the carpet.

"Now, Miss... Mrs... Ingrid. We don't have all day. As you may have heard, there's a killer out there and we need to catch him. So, if you could please tell us what you know."

Ingrid stares at them a while longer, a soft smile on her face, before sighing and leaning back in her chair.

"Fine, I'll talk. It was Friday night last. I was already up. I don't sleep a lot. Just sort of potter around the flat. Anyway, it was gone four when I was looking out of the window. The town looks so nice from here. All the lights. Reminds me of London. Before..." she trails off and looks at McNally's shoes.

"So you saw the attack?" Dawson continues.

"Yes, yes. I was looking out when I saw a young boy walk past my window. Stumbling about. I laughed. I thought it was quite funny. I remember being that young and drunk. Running around with my Harry and-"

"Ingrid!"

"Yes, sorry. Well, I returned my gaze to the town and was just standing up to go to bed when I looked down on to the street again. There was a hooded black figure standing over that poor boy. He had a knife in his hand. He stepped over the body and ran. I never saw anything like it."

"What direction did he run in?"

"Back towards the bridge. Down Spruce Lane. I couldn't see him once he passed the accountants. It was too dark and my view was blocked by my lovely neighbours."

"Why didn't you ring the police?"

"The police?" Ingrid laughs. "The police are horrible people. They were the reason I lost my Harry. They took him away and when he came back he was never the same."

"When we approached you at our door-to-door interviews you said you were sleeping, is that correct?"

"Yes. It was a darker officer. Lovely, long black hair. But I wanted nothing to do with her. Bitch. Her, so good looking, and decided to join a vile gang like the police. Well I ought to tell-"

"Ingrid, if you don't stay focused we're going to arrest you for perverting the course of justice."

Ingrid falls silent and returns her attention to the fireplace. McNally follows her gaze to a wedding picture sitting on the wooden mantelpiece. Although years old and faded by the sun, it was clearly Ingrid in the white dress.

"Is that your husband, Ingrid?"

Dawson's head snaps to the right but McNally gives him a quiet 'shh.'

"It was. My Harry."

"If you don't mind me asking, what happened? Did you get divorced?"

It's now Ingrid's head that snaps in McNally's direction.

"Divorced? We were in love. Why the hell would we ever get divorced?"

"I'm sorry. Did he die?"

Fresh tears burn in Ingrid's eyes.

"We had such a lovely life in London. That's where we met, you know? Me, a receptionist. Learning shorthand and stealing a few cocktails at the weekend. Him, a banker. My boss. Showering me with gifts. We got married three weeks after meeting. We were so in love. We travelled the world. Him and I. We were so happy."

Her soft nostalgic tone is replaced with a hardened spit.

"Then, one day, the police were at our door. They took him into custody and he didn't return. Said he was at the centre of some trouble. GBH. Drugs. Burglary. None of it true. I told them. He told them. But they wouldn't listen. He was locked up for years. Finally, they arrested the bastard who was truly guilty of the crimes. They

101

released my Harry. But it was too late. He had a brain tumour. He died a few months later. In my arms."

She starts openly crying now, burying her face in her hands.

"Ingrid, I'm so sorry," McNally reaches over and taps her on the leg. "But do you know what? The person who took Harry's place deserved to be there. He caused another man pain. He caused yourself pain. And now, someone else is doing that. Stephen could have died. We believe that his attacker may have killed someone else. We need to find out details about him. What did he look like? You're our first witness. We need your information. Stephen doesn't know a lot. He got attacked from behind and passed out shortly before the offender left. You're the best case of evidence we've got so far. Please, if it's not too much trouble, describe him."

Ingrid stares at McNally a while longer. She sighs and blows her nose on her sleeve.

"He was taller than Stephen. Probably just over six foot. Very skinny. Wore a black baggy hoody and dark jeans with trainers. His hood was up. But he stood there a few moments after he hurt Stephen. I believe he almost regretted it. Maybe took a moment to reflect on what he did. Please find him. I don't want anyone else getting hurt."

"We will," Dawson nods his head.

Ingrid's eyes burn towards Dawson, her face a mix of alarm as if she didn't see him sitting there.

"I'm sure you will. Go arrest the next person on the street and charge them. Go on! Out of my flat. I said out!"

She stands and starts shooing them out with her hands. McNally begins to thank her, but before he can ask her to contact them if she remembers anything else, the door of flat 12C is slammed in their faces. The pair look at each other for one last time, before pressing the button for the lift.

"She really didn't like you," McNally laughs.

"We can't use that as a witness statement. She's deluded, man!"

"But why make it up?"

"Why call us when you hate police that much?"

"I think it was something to do with Roberta Mills' article. I saw it sitting on the counter in the kitchen. I think she felt emotion for Stephen and knew that she saw what happened. Well, the aftermath of it anyway."

Dawson raises his eyebrows. Budds and McNally were right. However, it was still mid-morning. Maybe there were more reliable witnesses waiting for them in the station.

"Say what you want," he laughs. "She's still crazy."

"I think she's very bitter and confused. Maybe she's alone since she moved here from London, after the death of her husband. But, I believe her."

Dawson snorts in disgust and holds the door out into Nelson Street open for McNally.

"Well, even if we can believe her, all we know is that he was tall and slim. That doesn't narrow it down."

"Yes, but she described what he was wearing. Now we know what to look for when patrolling through CCTV."

Dawson nods in approval as they slump into the unmarked cop car.

"Good going, McNally. Maybe you'll have my job after all."

CHAPTER 21:

I'm fuming with anger. I can't believe she'd say something like that. I slam the door behind me and jump down the stairs, two at a time. I need to cool off. But as I reach for the front door, Mum's on my back straight away.

"Where are you going?"

"Out."

"James, you know how I feel about you going out at this time of night. Look at you. You're shaking. I hope you weren't going to drive."

"No. I was going to go a walk."

"A walk?" she screams. "Get in here."

Mum grabs me and pulls me into the kitchen.

With a steaming cup of hot chocolate in my hands, I start to calm down.

"Say when," she smiles as she starts to spill the mini marshmallows into my cup.

When a few dozen marshmallows sink into the cloudy liquid I tell her to stop, but she won't. After several attempts, I move my cup away, laughing, causing the remainder of the mallows to spill over the counter.

"Now look at the mess you've made," Mum laughs before scooping them up and popping them into her mouth.

We laugh a while longer, but probably on cue, the noise of the toilet flushing can be heard above our heads. We return our eyes from the ceiling and gaze at each other a minute, the same half smile painted on both of our faces. That lasted long.

"Want to talk about it?" Mum whispers, placing her hand on my arm.

"Not really, it's just stupid as usual," I sip from the fresh cup and let the liquid warm my insides from the hollowness.

Mum gets up and turns the tap on. It splutters to life and starts to fill the sink. She then progresses to turn the microwave dial to five minutes. The plate in the middle starts to rotate with its signature hum. Even if Stacey does have her ears pressed to the tiles in the bathroom, which I wouldn't be surprised if she did, it'll be hard to hear us now.

"She just infuriates me. So much," I start, placing the cup on the table in fear of spilling the contents.

"What's it about this time?"

"I told her that I skipped class today-"

"James!"

"I know, I know. But I was safe, I swear! Tuesdays are awful. I have Maths first thing for an hour and then have nothing but Geology and study hall for the rest of the day. I just decided to come home. I didn't loiter about any side streets, if that's what you're thinking. I came home and made a start on my coursework-"

"Which you could do in study hall."

"Yeah, I know, Mum. But if I go to study hall, then I have to go to Geology. It's just so boring. And the kids in the class below are so immature. They started laughing hysterically when the teacher was talking about dikes."

Mum gives me a peculiar look and I explain the rock terminology.

"I just wanted to come home. I told Deans I was going and he didn't have a problem with it. He even offered to drive me."

Mum stands up to turn the tap off before the sink overflows.

"I'd prefer it if Mr Deans took on a bit more responsibility. I know you've always got on well, but he could let you get away with murder. If that was any other of his kids, I'm sure they'd be expelled. Just be careful, James. Anyway, what does this have to do with…?"

She points to the roof and mouths the spelling of Stacey's name. I lower my voice.

"She obviously thought I was going off with some other girl. Seeing someone behind her back. Then asking her over for sloppy seconds."

Mum rolls her eyes and messes my hair.

"Don't let her get into your head. It's *her* insecurities that she has to deal with. She shouldn't have to pass them on to you. You're doing nothing wrong. Just stand your ground. You're forgetting where you've got your stubbornness from."

She flexes her arms and pretends to box her imaginary opponent as she glides out of the room.

"You're a muppet, Mum," I laugh.

She's right. I boil the kettle again to bring Stacey up some hot chocolate. She's sitting on the end of my bed, arms folded, when I enter the room.

"I brought you up some ho-"

"So, go crying to your Mum again, yeah?"

Stacey's chin is sticking so far out of her head it looks like, if touched, it would snap off.

"What? No, I wanted to go a wa-"

"So mature, aren't you? Running to Mummy."

"Stacey, I told you already. Mum's so worked up about these recent attacks, she doesn't want me-"

"Oh, her precious James wouldn't have to worry about them, now would he? He's so perfect, why would anyone ever want to hurt him?"

"Stacey, grow up. I didn't go to-"

"And what were you talking about anyway? I could hear you, you know? Talking about dykes. Going downstairs after a row to talk to your mum about lesbians, are you? You two are far too close. What you do when she's at work in this house is more my business than hers."

"Stacey, what the hell are yo-"

"I bet it's just a big joke. Isn't it? You and your mum. Laughing about me. Oh, ha-ha, Stacey's at college and I've brought two girls home with me for a threesome. They say they're lesbians, but clearly not since I got them into my bed."

"You're being ridiculous."

"Oh really? When I came over, your bed wasn't made. What else aren't you telling me?"

107

"I never make my bloody bed. I was in it all day doing coursework anyway."

"I'm sure. You just lie your way out of it just-"

We're interrupted by my phone ringing.

"Don't you dare answer th-"

"Teddy, boy. What's up?"

I flop myself down into my beanbag and avert my eyes from Stacey's ajar mouth. She flicks her head sideways and glares at my door.

"Not a lot, mate. Here, were you talking to some detective bloke. I forget his name."

"Dawson?"

"That's the one. Yeah, he's just after ringing me. Asking me if I was with you the other night. Took me a while to remember. I was wasted, man."

We both laugh.

"Yeah. That was the night that Begley boy got attacked. He's interviewing everyone in school. He must've wanted to follow up on my alibi. Cheers for letting them know anyway, pal."

"Yeah, no probs. He seems a bit shady, this guy. He was asking me all these side questions and wording things weirdly. Anyway, he tried to get me to admit that you were staying at mine that night. Probably another mind game. I told him you disappeared home without a goodbye to anyone. Probably vomiting your dinner up in the men's and didn't want to admit defeat."

He bursts into laughter again, but this time, it's one-sided. I stare across the room, trying to look as casual as possible in front of Stacey and make sure Teddy can't hear my heart beating in my throat.

"Yeah, mate. Something like that. Well, cheers for helping. Hopefully that's the last we hear of him."

"What are you doing this-"

But I hang up before I get to hear the rest of the invite. Stacey returns her gaze to me and instantly knows something's wrong. Shit. What the fuck am I going to do now?

CHAPTER 22:

DI Dawson hangs up the phone and returns to the tight dark cupboard that the station calls a studio. So, Kingston didn't stay at his friend's flat that night the Begley boy got attacked. And he has no alibi except his bedroom walls for the other attacks, he thinks to himself. Interesting. McNally budges over a smidge so Dawson can fit his huge thighs behind the cramped desk. As they both leer over the double monitors in front of them, Dawson has an idea.

"Let's start looking for someone in particular, shall we?"

"Sir?"

"I think we may have a lead. James Kingston. A few kids at the school said he's a bit odd. Ditches class. Shifty eyes. Doesn't really pal up with anyone. When I interviewed him, he either said he was alone or, as I've just found out, has given a false alibi. Seemed very on edge. Let me get my notes and we'll see where he was throughout the night. We already know that a few of the pubs paired up with where Stephen was."

A quarter of an hour later, the DI is back spinning through CCTV footage of The Fork and Spoons Bar.

"Why do they call it 'Spoons' anyway? Why not 'The Fork,' I think it sounds loads bette-"

"Shut up, McNally."

"I was just saying, sir."

"Well, don't. Look at this!"

The two officers return their concaved shoulders to the screens. Dawson presses the fast forward button numerous times.

"Look," he points to a blurry image on the screen. "That's Stephen."

A fuzzy faced Stephen is standing at the bar, ordering a host of drinks by the looks of how long his mouth has been in the barmaid's ear. Finally, she walks away to get his orders and he visibly checks her out, before sheepishly looking around to his girlfriend, sitting with a few people three tables behind.

"Looks like the sneak was looking for more than just a few beers."

Stephen gazes at the barmaid as she pours him his drinks. As he goes to pay her, he leans in and starts talking again. She looks like she's having none of it and pulls the note out of his tight fist. Stephen shrugs off the encounter, grabs his drinks and turns around only to spill everything over the boy behind him.

"Him! That's Kingston!"

Dawson points at James, who looks down his own front, appalled. Stephen mimes apologetically, but James just shrugs him off and marches to the other side of the bar, pulling out his phone and jumping up on a stool. Stephen's girlfriend looks like she's seen the sleazing with the barmaid and marches out of the pub, friends in tow. Stephen hurries after them.

"Now look..."

James is swaying on the stool, looking at the door swinging shut behind Stephen. He glances at his phone and types for a few seconds before replacing it in his pocket. Looking around the packed pub, he slides towards the back door, out into the smoking garden and out of sight.

"See!"

"Do you really think that that's enough?"

"His friends are at that other table, look."

Dawson points to the top right-hand side of the screen, at a few rowdy boys playing pool.

"He doesn't return."

McNally stares at the screen and nods approvingly.

"I know someone spilling their drink all over you can annoy you, but stabbing someone?" McNally shifts uncomfortably, unintentionally rubbing his leg off Dawson's.

"There could be an ulterior motive. He never mentioned seeing Stephen at all. Never mind physically bumping into him. Did you see how on edge he was as soon as the encounter happened? And slipping out the back door without saying goodbye to his friends? I think he's hiding something."

Dawson picks up the DVD containing CCTV footage of The Mag's Pub. Five minutes later, his thick fingers are on the screen again.

"Look, there's the lads he was hanging around with. And James is nowhere to be seen. It looks like I'll be paying another visit to Mr Kingston."

CHAPTER 23:

Roberta rings the doorbell of number six and waits patiently on the welcome mat. The door inches open. She sees it's on a chain and an elderly man peaks half of his face under it.

"Yes?"

"Hi, sir. My name is Rober-"

"I know who you are."

And with that, he slams the door shut. Roberta stands opened mouthed and disgusted a while longer, before giving the doorbell another press. This has happened before in her long career, of course, but never so abruptly. Moments later, she rings again. After her fourth attempt, she hears the chain getting ripped to the side and the oak door flies open. Silhouetted against the hall light is Gemma's father.

"Mr Norris. Hi. My na-"

"Do you people have no shame? We have asked the press to respect our privacy-"

"And I do respect that, sir. But I would just like-"

"Well you obviously don't or you wouldn't be here begging for an exclusive in my front garden!"

"-to let you know of the success of the Stephen Begley story."

Mr Norris opens his mouth to protest, but frowns and exhales, his chest visibly deflating.

"Success?"

Now is Roberta's chance.

"Yes, the police haven't told you?"

"Erm… No. The police haven't told us anything."

"Well, since my exclusive with Stephen Begley, they have had several phone-ins which have led to the investigation of a couple of suspects. It seemed to jog people's memories. Get a bit of sympathy going around our community. I know we have tried to contact you on several occasions, but now that you know that the press *are* here to help you, would you agree to an interview?"

Mr Norris still looks at Roberta with his teeth clenched.

"Wait here."

He slams the door shut, leaving Roberta with only the breeze and a jump of fright at the sound.

"Any luck?" Julie looks up from her screen as Roberta shuffles into her cubicle.

"Zero."

Roberta returns to her desk and blows out a sigh, momentarily lifting her fringe off her head.

"Couldn't get through the parents again?"

"Well, the dad did budge, actually. It's Gemma. She's dead set on not speaking to me. Said she doesn't want her name in the papers any more than it already is."

"Maybe you should leave it at that. Hopefully, with these new suspects, someone will be prosecuted."

"Yeah, I guess. I just can't shake the feeling that there's something wrong. Something obvious. How could the both of them not see his face? Surely we should know a bit more than his height for Christ's sake. Especially this far into the investigation."

"It's only been a fortnight, Rob. Give it time."

And with that, Julie picks up her landline and gets to work on her roadworks story. A typical journo, Roberta thinks. Just enough empathy to ask the questions, but selfish enough to go back to her own story when she's ran out of answers. Roberta picks up the double-page spread on Stephen, now days old and reads and re-reads her print. She's missing something. But what?

CHAPTER 24:

I wake up with a start. Nightmares again. A small slither of light intrudes itself through the curtains into my room and I glance at my watch. Nearly 7am. I'll have to be up anyway. Might as well be first one to the shower. The voices in my head and the scratches on the door weren't as bad last night. I think I got a solid two or three hours sleep. Better than most nights.

Grabbing my mouldy damp towel, I make my way across the landing. The old pipes grumble as the shower, no stronger than a light drizzle, trickles into life. When I'm finished undressing, I wave my hand under the water. Still freezing. I lean against the sink and gaze at myself in the mirror. The dark rings under my eyes give away my sleepless nights. I stare right into my eyes and get flashbacks of the light going out in Derek's. His face as he looked up at me. His gasps as I drove my weapon into his stomach. I shudder, and not from the cold.

As the mirror starts to steam up, I climb into the shower. Turning the temperature up as far as I can without physically burning myself. Almost as if the hot water will purify me and my sins. Washing them down the drain with the dirty water. I hear movement from the rooms either side. My solace won't last long. I reach for the shampoo bottle.

Moments later, I feel a cold spell hitting my head. I gasp in surprise and wait for it to return to my boiling temperature. Why did that happen? Usually that only occurs when you flush the toilet or something. I wipe the soap and shampoo out of my eyes and gaze around me, making sure I'm definitely alone. Content with my privacy, I return my attention to my cleaning routine. But I gasp once more. There it is again, the cold water. This time it lasts longer. I jump away almost impulsively and that's when I see it. Blood! Blood at my feet. All over my body. I start to hyperventilate. I gaze up at the shower nozzle. It continues to spit out the red thick liquid and I scream.

I'm jolted awake. Breathing heavily. Sweating profusely. It was just a dream. I look around at the familiarity of my dark room.

"Just a dream, just a dream," I whisper to myself, trying to calm my racing heart.

My watch tells me it's only gone four. I still have another few hours of this. It seems like the scratching at the door has stopped. The voices in my head aren't able to shout louder than my own thoughts, reverting back to my dream. Even the posters on the walls aren't judging me now. I lie back in bed and wrap my arms around my legs, shivering freely, but don't reach for my sweat soaked blankets, which fell onto the floor in my outburst. I try desperately to silently cry myself back to sleep.

CHAPTER 25:

God, I don't want to be here. With everything going on right now, why would I want to be in the middle of town in this shitty club with Stacey's awful friends? Revolving on the bar stool, I try to search for someone I can actually have a conversation with, but have to stop. Too many tequilas. I gaze over at Stacey, hugging Maisy and getting her hair caught in Maisy's birthday badge. She looks beautiful tonight. Her long black dress, slit right down one leg, gets me instantly aroused. And why wouldn't it? We haven't had sex in weeks. She's been so cagey with me recently because I wouldn't tell her why I acted so weird after I hung up the phone with Teddy. I played it off cool, but she nagged and nagged until I snapped and we had a row.

The next day in school was fun. DI Dawson dragging me out of Maths class, *again*. Cemented into the interrogation seat in Deans' office that I grew to love so well. Not anymore. I had discomfort all over my ass after getting up from the hour-long interview. I pleaded my innocence, saying I must have got my dates mixed up. I did stay at Teddy's another night. I must've went home that night. Dawson didn't buy it. He said he'd ring my parents. I told him they didn't see or hear me come in. He kept asking me if I wanted to admit to something. I refused. He told me there's CCTV footage of me leaving the bar straight after Stephen. I told him I felt sick and wanted to go home. I had and have no motive to attack anyone, never mind some kid I barely know. I know it sounds bad. All I'm doing is fucking another girl, but I don't want to admit it. I don't know if it's a conscience thing, or because it's Lydia, or I'm scared of Stacey or of my parents finding out. My head's a mess. And this double gin isn't helping.

I take a quick glance at my phone. Still no reply from Lydia. We haven't seen each other since that night. Well, no. That's a lie. We've seen each other in school. But we don't make eye contact. She's texted me drunk looking for a quick ride and I've either been busy or not in the mood. She's probably playing games with me because when I text, she doesn't reply either. It's kind of always been like this. Back and forth. Only really works when it suits both of us. Not that it's ever a good idea to go through with it.

I'm brought back to reality with a punch on the shoulder. I turn to see Teddy standing, arms outstretched and the same cheesy grin on his face.

"About bloody time, mate," I laugh and give him a hug.

"I know, I know. I'm late." Teddy rolls his eyes. He's always late. Moderately more late than usual this time. It has gone midnight.

"But..." he points to a girl coming out of the bathroom. She smiles timidly as she fights her way through the crowd towards us. All hair, no brains, I bet. Of course there was a girl involved.

"Tinder," he whispers in my ear before turning and kissing the girl on the top of the head.

"Hi, I'm Olivia," she extends her hand to me.

Teddy scrunches up his face, purses his lips and nods his head as he stands behind her. She is hot, I guess. If you're into big tits and no ass.

"Teddy, nice to see you. It's been ages."

Oh, here comes the Ice Queen, I nearly say out loud, turning around to see Stacey's fake smile. Must've saw Olivia and skirted straight over. They have their introductions and make small chit-chat whilst I order two beers, Olivia isn't drinking. She's got church tomorrow. I nod in fake approval and give side eyes to Teddy. He still seems pretty confident.

"Aren't you getting me a drink?"

I stare at Stacey's cocktail. She can't have even taken two sips from it.

"Umm…"

"Well anyway," she flips her head back, hitting me up the face with her blonde locks. "I hear you all had a mad night the other week. Around your flat? This one didn't make it back to mine until tea time the next day."

She wraps her arms around me and giggles. Looking innocent. Her talent. No-one can see the death grip she has, digging her polished nails into my side.

"Yeah, the poor sod was sick all over himself, had to go home early," Teddy explodes into laughter again, wrapping his own arm around Olivia, who pulls a polite face, but can't hide her disgust.

Shit. Teddy!

I widen my eyes at him, but it's too late.

"Oh, I was under the impression that he came home with you that night?"

"James? No, no. That detective bloke thought that too. I don't know why. Must've been shagging away."

Teddy raises his hand for a high five and I groan. Teddy hates Stacey. He lives to wind her up. Stacey sucks her teeth, smiles at Olivia and excuses herself. Pulling away, she marches towards the exit.

"Cheers, pal," I shake my head at Teddy before chasing after her. We're almost at the door when I grab her hand.

"Babe-"

But before I know it, she has me against the wall, her free hand around my throat.

"Don't. You. *Dare*! 'Babe' me," she spits, her eyes wide.

I grab her hand with both of mine and manage to pull her off, but not before she throws the rest of her drink in my face.

I scream aloud. My eyes!

After I can half see again, I stumble out of the bar and down Chessington Street, knowing Stacey far too well. There she is, her usual spot. Waiting outside the statue of the woman dragging her two kids along, half way through a curry chip.

"How are you so good at making an absolute fool out of me, James Kingston?"

"Me? Make a fool out of you? You must be joking. You threw your fucking drink over me, Stacey. Everyone in the bar seen."

"Oh, who cares about them? Who cares what anyone thinks?"

Stacey's tears are mixing in with the runny curry, currently dripping from the tin and over the ground.

"Listen, I just didn't want to tell you that I went home. I was in a bad mood after we fought-"

"So why didn't you answer my texts? My calls?"

"I just wanted to teach you a lesson."

"Teach me a lesson? You had me worried sick! That Stephen boy could've been you, James!"

"Now don't give me that bullshit, you didn't even know that boy had been attacked until after I left your house."

"Yeah, well... It could still happen. You out drinking with your friends, making an ass out of yourself. And I could never see you again. Me at home crying, worrying about you and you out shagging anything that moves."

"Teddy's just saying that to annoy you."

"Then why did you come in the clothes from the night before, James? Why didn't you get changed before you came to mine? And why didn't you drive over?"

"Why would I come in a different pair of clothes when I said I was staying at Teddy's? And why would I drive? For a start, I was well over the limit, and that would completely defeat the illusion that I was staying at Teddy's."

"You're impossible. Can't even admit to your own mistakes. I don't know why I stay with you. Honestly..."

An hour later we're still fighting. Same stupid argument, just different locations. Moving from the statue to the taxi, from my front garden to my kitchen and finally from my room to my bed. During a lull in the argument, we're in darkness, but I can feel her sitting up. The fight out of her. Sobbing uncontrollably. Hunched over. I get a stab of guilt. I roll around from my side and try to comfort her, but she pushes me away. I try and pull her into a hug but she won't budge.

"Why don't you love me?"

"What? Stacey, of course I love you. Do you really think I'd be staying with you if I didn't?"

Oops. Wrong thing to say. I can almost see the flames behind her eyes as she looks up.

"What's that supposed to mean? Hard work am I? I'm sorry for loving you and caring about you whilst all you do is go out and slut about. Shagging every other girl you see."

"Oh, grow up, will you? It's the same old-"

"Grow up? *You* grow up, James. You go out all the time with your mates doing God only knows what. I ask for one night. *One night*. I ask you to my best friend's birthday party-"

"Best friend? You've known Maisy for less than two weeks, I wouldn't go that far."

"-and all you do is sit like a miserable bastard at the bar. Not speaking to anyone. You barely said happy birthday to Maisy. And you didn't so much as look at me all night."

"Are you fucking joking?"

I snap. It's taken a lot longer than usual, the alcohol oozing out my patience. But here we go.

"You went on and on about this party. Forcing me to go. Of course I wouldn't want to go. I knew no one. The only reason I came is because I knew that if I didn't, you would've fallen out with me. And for what? Me to show up and you not even take me on. You didn't say two words to me all night until you saw another girl there. Jealous of her, were you? Yeah, that's my motive. I stay faithful all those nights I'm out alone, and then when I'm out with you, I try and cheat on you, right to your face. And with my best mate's date. That's me isn't it? You really are a psychotic, manipulative bit-"

The rest of my insult is lost.

Through the darkness, I don't see the first fist hit me right on my temple. The second connects with my bottom lip. My bed turns into a sea of limbs. Stacey drunkenly hurling her fists and feet at me. Anything to make a connection. I grab both of her wrists and roll over on top of her to calm her down.

"Get off me! Get the fuck off me!"

"Are you going to calm down?"

"I mean it, get the fuck off me or I'm calling your parents."

"Okay, well stop."

I relax my grip on her wrists and start to move away, but she kicks me straight in the stomach. I double over in pain as she starts attacking me again. She climbs on top of me to get better angles.

"Ger-off" I grumble through pain and swipe my arm towards her, pushing her off me.

And with that, she's flying through the air. I hear the bang of her back and head against my wardrobe and floor. She gasps and the crying instantly stops, being replaced with shock.

"Stace – are you okay? I'm sorry but you really hurt me. Have I hu-"

"Don't talk to me," she gets up and starts packing her things, half blind from the drink and half blind from the darkness of my room. The fresh tears aren't helping. I can hear her shivering from the sobs. I turn on my sidelight and crawl out of bed to comfort her. She's having none of it.

Less than 15 minutes later, her taxi is reversing out of my drive. I watch it from the front door window, before turning around to see Mum peering at me from the top of the stairs.

"What the hell has been going on, James?"

CHAPTER 26:

Dawson sits up in bed, swerving his heavy legs around and delicately placing his bare feet on to the fuzzy carpet. He presses his hands into his face and groans.

"You're getting old," his wife mumbles next to him, still half asleep.

As he gets ready for the long day ahead, he thinks back on the past few weeks, cursing himself. How has history repeated itself? The quiet town of Rong Valley plastered over every newspaper in the country. *Again.* Local hotels packed to the brim with journalists from around the world, trying to get their say on the juicy case.

What case? He almost grumbles out loud. They have no suspects apart from James Kingston, who, although Dawson hates to admit it, has no motive. He may have no alibi and a fitted description, but they need more than that. And since none of the victims had any form of their attacker's DNA or other such evidence on them or around the crime scene, they're still clutching at straws. The only solid witness, if you could call her that, was Ingrid Bloom, who, in Dawson's opinion, had been little to no help. Even with the description of the attacker's outfit, all CCTV footage around the town couldn't trace him or his movements on the night of Stephen's attack. After a particularly hard day, Dawson had personally went to local shops and other amenities and gave them hell about not keeping their CCTV up to date. They shrugged back, telling him the town didn't see a lot of crime apart from local kids pinching a few chocolate bars now and again. Dawson had driven around all night after, but hated to admit that they were right.

And now, moving into week three, the topic of '*The Return of Rong Valley's Teen Killer*' had fallen completely out of the press. The only thing keeping the story alive were a few social media pages devoted to Derek French, striving the community to be vigilant in finding his killer. As for trying to link the victims, they had no such luck. Apart from the school, none of them were in the same friendship circles, afterschool activities, not even in the same PE classes.

"We need something big soon," Dawson tells himself, whilst pouring his first cup of coffee of the day.

And with that, his mobile vibrates ferociously on the kitchen table.

"McNally, please tell me we have something?"

"We do, sir."

Dawson tilts his head back and quietly blesses himself.

"We've just had an arrest this morning. A couple had too many drinks and things got a bit... Er... Physical."

Dawson stares at his tired reflection in the kitchen window, waiting for the connections. None come.

"McNally, what the hell does this have to do wi-"

"Two teenagers. Rong Valley High. One kid we've seen before. And we have reason to believe he's linked to Derek French."

Dawson smirks as he takes a sip of his coffee, suddenly tasting that little bit better.

"We've got him!"

The hustle and bustle of the station is more dramatic than other mornings. Word has somehow gotten out about the arrest and the phones are ringing all over the office. Dawson marches his way through the bee-hive of people and straight for Interview Room 1. The claustrophobia in the room is worsened by the large desk, which occupies the majority of the whitewashed space. It makes it almost impossible to climb in and out of behind each side of the desk without sucking your stomach in.

Johnny Kitson finds a way of swinging on his chair anyway.

McNally and Dawson struggle to fit themselves comfortably opposite him. After a few seconds of discomfort and the untangling of legs, they settle into starting the interview.

"Are you sure you don't want a lawyer present?" McNally tries sweet talking Kitson. Always the good cop.

"Don't need one, do I?"

"Well, I don't know. That's for you to answer, I suppose."

"Don't want one."

"We can supply you with one if you don't have the money."

"Got fuck all to do with money, mate. Just know I didn't do nout wrong."

That's when Dawson interjects.

"Look, *mate.* We'd appreciate it if you would help us with our enquiries. We will not accept abusive or harsh language. Do you understand?"

Kitson rolls his eyes and returns to staring at his fingernails. He's dressed in the mandatory grey fleece and tracksuit bottoms, not dissimilar to the outfit the uniforms had taken from him for evidence. His greasy hair still has fragments of blood in it and his clenched jaw stands prominent on the rat-like features of his face. Dawson almost sneers with disgust. Kitson was of no use to Dawson when he interviewed him at the school. Bunking class to smoke in the toilets, that's where they said they had found him. Of course, just because he doesn't have an interest in education, he couldn't be judged on that. But he seemed to have had solid alibis on the nights in question. Saying he was out drinking on the streets with friends, naming them all and daring Dawson to follow it up. Not caring about being charged with loitering or drinking in a public place. He knew there were more important matters than a few teenagers drinking cider on the corner. He's not stupid, Dawson had thought to himself then, and repeats it now. So why is he acting like it?

"What happened last night?" McNally asks.

Kitson shrugs and begins biting his filthy nails, staring into the corner.

"If you can tell us what happened, in your own words, we'll be able to piece the puzzle together."

Nothing.

"Where were you drinking?"

Dawson's voice booms through the empty room, making quite a contrast to McNally's soft tone. He almost saw Kitson jump with fright. But still nothing.

"Look, *mate*. You can start talking now or we can throw you in the cells for a few hours? Maybe that will loosen your tongue?"

Kitson's eyes rest on Dawson's and he smirks. Taking his finger out of his mouth, he spits out a nail. Everyone watches it hit the wall to his left, and fall to the floor, almost as if in slow motion.

"What you wanna know, then?"

"Everything."

"'bout what?"

"You know full well, now stop wasting our time."

"Alright, alright. Me and Emily were just havin' a laugh and that. Then one thing led to another and I might've hit her. By accident, of course. I didn't even know it were her. I was really drunk. She started crying and I apologised, but she left the street corner. Phoned the cops. And now here we are."

He spreads out his arms, resumes swinging on his chair and stares at them, lips pursed.

"Why did you fall out?"

"Don't 'member."

"Why did you hit her?"

"Don't 'member."

"Where were you in the early hours of September 12th."

"Don't…" Kitson eyes Dawson curiously, visibly taken aback. "…'member."

"You don't *member* the night that Derek French was killed? It's been headline news. I asked you where you were that night, back in the school, *member* that? You told me you were out with your mates. Drinking on the street. From what I *member*, you said you were home for about… When? One? … 2am perhaps? Well, when we interviewed Emily Long, she said that her and Derek had both left the park just before four. So, Mr Kitson. Where were you?"

130

He has gone quiet again. Staring at Dawson, chewing the inside of his mouth. After a few minutes, the same sickly smile returns to his face.

"You don't seriously think I did that, do you? You're mad. Away with the fairies."

"How long have you been seeing Emily Long for, Johnny?"

Kitson shrugs his shoulders and stops swinging on his chair. He shifts the itchy jumper about and his eyes move around the small room. This is the bit that Dawson loves about Interview Room 1. Nowhere to look. Nowhere to hide. You'd go mad in here. He thrives in watching them squirm.

"'bout a week or so."

"That a fact? Because Miss Long has told us that you've been seeing her for quite some time. April, was it? Some girl called Louise's party. Am I right?"

Again with the shrug.

"And there was a falling out at that party. Was there not? Between you and a certain Derek French?"

The penny has dropped, and so has Kitson's mouth.

"That were just a drunken scrap. Nothing. He saw me kissin' her. I got a slap. My own fault. I were drunk. Deserved it. Realise now I did wrong. We hadn't spoke since."

"But your relationship with Emily continued. Am I right?"

"Well... Yeah. But on the down low. He didn't know. No one knows. So I have no-"

"Seem to be quite the charmer, Mr Kitson."

"Eh?"

131

"Emily has said you've been in constant contact with her since. Messages. Snapchats. The lot. Said you've been bugging her for months. Asking her to break up with Derek. Sending her pictures of yourself. Some a bit too revealing for my taste, I must say. Seems she turned you down, didn't she?"

"No! We was still fucking even before he died."

"So *'a week or so'* has been upgraded to a few months, now. Am I right?"

"Lost track of time is all."

"And as you said, you were in a physical relationship?"

He gives half a nod.

"So why didn't Emily break up with Derek?"

"Said she loved him. Didn't know what she were doing with me. Just a bit of fun whilst he was off with the lads."

"So you took matters into your own hands?"

"What? No!"

"Decided that if you got him out of the picture that you could be together, am I right?"

"I never-"

"So, let's say you were stalking Emily that night. Or were you actually stalking Derek?"

"I weren't stalking nobody-"

"You followed them into the park. You saw what they were doing and you were angry, weren't you?"

"No! I swear I never-"

"So you killed him. Now there's a gap in Emily's life that you want to fill."

"You have it all wrong!"

Kitson slams his fists on the table, spit flying from his mouth and landing on both of the officer's faces.

"I never touched him. I were in bed, I swear. I didn't even see 'em at all that night!"

"Phone records beg to differ. They showed that you were ringing and texting Emily after midnight."

"Yeah 'cause I were drunk. Looking for a quick fuck. I didn't stalk her. I didn't stalk anyone. I were ringing her, but we didn't meet up."

"How do you know Gemma Norris and Stephen Begley, Mr Kitson?"

"I have nothing to do with 'em. I know 'em from school, but that's it. Weren't my friends. Weren't in any of my classes. Saw 'em in the corridor a few times. That were it. Didn't even know their names 'til I saw 'em on news."

"So, you're saying that this violent outburst was an isolated incident?"

"Yeah! I swear."

"Let me take you a trip down memory lane, shall I? Three years ago, you were suspended for the last few weeks of school. Why?"

Kitson's eyes look like they're going to bulge out of his head.

"That got nout to do with anything. I-"

"You were suspended for threatening your classmate with a knife, am I right?"

"It were in workshop. We were messing about. He was my mate. We were having a laugh. I would never do anything like that to him, or to anyone. Teacher didn't find it funny. Neither did Mr Deans."

133

"I bet. So, if you don't mind, I'm going to terminate this interview. Leave it until lunch time, shall I? Maybe you'll be a bit more co-operative then."

Kitson's mouth is open but he's speechless. Dawson finds it hard to hide the smirk on his face as he closes the door to Interview Room 1.

"And that, McNally, is how it's done!"

CHAPTER 27:

Slowly closing the lid, I flush the toilet. A huge part of me wants to crawl up on the floor and hug the bowl, knowing full well I'll be back here in another few minutes when the next wave of nausea comes over me. But if Mum or Dad see me in this state, then I'll never hear the end of it. So, trudging myself to my room, I muffle myself in the duvet and wait for my stomach to settle. That's the third time I've been sick in the past half hour. What was I thinking taking shots of Tequila last night? I know they always leave me like this. I haven't heard from Stacey all morning. I doubt I will receive any form of contact for a while. If she hasn't texted by now, then she's giving me the silent treatment.

Thinking back on last night, my stomach takes another turn. To be fair, if she *was* completely in the wrong, then she would've texted by now. I did lie to her and I wasn't exactly Mr Party when I showed up at the club. Guilt starts to creep in and I moan. The fight wasn't my fault though. She attacked me. I was just defending myself by pushing her off me. I didn't know my own strength. That's what I keep telling myself as I scurry to the toilet again.

Half an hour later, Mum calls me to come downstairs. I creep down them in my tracksuit bottoms and last night's shirt. Every step making the pounding in my head worsen. I'm met at the front door by DI Dawson and groan. I have no time for his interrogations today.

"Detective?"

"James, we'd like you to come to the police station."

I roll my eyes.

"Look, I'm fed up with being the prime suspect. Can you stop wasting your time with me and actually get around to finding the real man who's attacked all these kids? I've got nothing more to say and my patience has basically ran out."

And with that, I start up the stairs again.

"Well, no, James. I've actually just had a really interesting chat with your parents."

I stop half way up the stairs.

"We've had a phone in this morning. Someone stating that you weren't where you said you were on the night of Stephen's attack, something we already knew. Your parents have just confirmed that you weren't here, either. You've been lying to us, James. And I want to get to the bottom of it. So, you can come quietly with me now or there's a nice policeman outside who will help me arrest you and take you into custody."

I turn around and see both Mum and Dad standing under the door frame to the living room. Mum crying and Dad with his arm around her. A new wave of nausea comes over me. I really am going to be sick again.

CHAPTER 28:

Emily Long sits in the more comfortable vicinity of Interview Room 2. She has a cooling cup of tea in front of her and looks a lot more innocent in her own clothes. A fresh stream of tears creep down the young girl's bruised face when Dawson and McNally delicately place themselves in front of her.

"Okay, Emily," McNally's soft voice is present again, as Dawson lets him take lead, considering the fragility of the situation. "We just want to take a full statement from you, okay? Then you're free to go home."

"Where is he?"

"Mr Kitson is in custody at the moment. We did question him, but there's a little more we'd like to ask, so we're giving him a short break before we resume the interview."

"Don't let that psychopath out. You hear me? He's bad news."

"Well, that's what we're trying to find out, Emily. So, if you could, in your own words, describe to us the events of last night."

Emily stares at McNally for a few moments, before sniffing and looking at her crossed hands on the table.

"Can I see my mum?"

"She's just outside. You can go home with her as soon as this statement is over and done with."

"Can she come in here with me?"

"Would you feel more comfortable if she were here?"

"Yes."

Dawson bites his tongue to hide his annoyance as McNally agrees and sends someone to fetch her mother from the waiting room. Moments later, they've resumed.

"We were at the corner of Larkin's Street. Johnny and his mates always hang around there. I don't know why. Think it's some sort of meeting point. Anyway, Smokey offered me some cider-"

"Smokey?" Dawson interjects.

"Yeah. Sorry, I don't know his real name."

"Okay... Carry on."

"Well, Smokey offered me some cider. It's the first time I've drank cider before-"

Dawson rolls his eyes. The worst thing about a young person's parents being present is the lies they spew out to protect their own asses. Mrs Long sits silently, holding her daughter's hand under the table and nods in approval every now and then.

"...Anyway, I remember Johnny coming up to me and kissing my neck. I kind of pushed him away. Not in an aggressive way or anything, just a sort of light shove. He kept coming forward and trying to kiss me and I just kept pushing him away. After the fourth or fifth time, I started to get annoyed and told him to stop it. He called me a slut and... and-"

Emily's hands clench and she gives her mum a side-glance.

"-and he started to get angry. Really mouthing off, calling me every name under the sun. So I started to walk away. I was gonna walk home and just leave it, but he followed me down the street. Roaring and shouting. I was so embarrassed. He shouted awful things. Hurtful, you know? Telling me he was glad Derek was dead and that he was nothing. I was too good for him because he was a worthless scumbag. He hated him. I had had a few drinks, so I turned around and told him to leave me alone. Telling him that I didn't want to see him anymore because he was vile. Abusive. I was so angry, I don't remember a lot of what I said, sorry. I turned and started crying, half running. But when I got to the corner, I felt a hit to the back of my head."

"An object?"

"No, like a fist. I fell to the ground and turned to see him over me. He didn't look like himself. He was so angry. He looked like a completely different person."

The tears are now flowing more freely in both Emily and her mother's eyes.

"He kicked me in the stomach and called me a slut again. I remember screaming and crying and trying to get back up. But every time I did, he just kept hitting me. Finally, one of his mates must've seen us. He ran over and grabbed him and pulled him away. I managed to get myself up and made it home."

She blubbers into her mother's blouse as she pulls her in for a hug. Her shoulders caving in and releasing the last of her confidence and energy.

"I'm sorry to hear that, Emily," McNally nods, his eyes on the pair.

"Just a few questions then, Miss Long."

Emily looks taken aback as Dawson clears his throat.

"When did all this take place?"

"Um… I don't know," she sniffs. "About half 11 last night?"

"So why did it take you so long to come forward? Why only this morning?"

"I got home and just got into bed and cried. Mum found me this morning and phoned the ambulance."

"And I'm glad she did," McNally widens his eyes at Dawson as a silent *'shut up.'* "It's good you're okay and things didn't get worse. We want to let you know of all the facilities that are availa-"

"Just one more moment, DS McNally. I have a few more questions, if you could answer them please?"

Emily's sniffs again and wipes her snottery nose with the back of her fake tan stained hand.

"When did you start having a physical relationship with Mr Kitson?"

Emily's eyes widen as she stares at the detective.

"Um... I don't know what you're talking about. We kissed last week when I was drunk, but-"

"You told our uniformed officers that you have been seeing Mr Kitson since April, did you not?"

"No. Ah... No, no such thing."

"Mrs Long, could I ask you to please step out of the room for a moment. I need a word," Dawson sighs heavily.

"She is physically shook up, for Christ's sake. Now, I know you are only doing your job, but *she's* the victim here!"

Mrs Long's face is inches from Dawson's as she fights to take her daughter home.

"I appreciate that, Mrs Long. But we *are* in the middle of a very important investigation that I think your daughter has had some involvement in. We would just like to keep her in for another few hours, then she's free to leave. However, you saw her in there. She has clammed up and clearly doesn't want to speak about certain events in your presence-"

"Because she has nothing to say! She hasn't been seeing that Kitson boy. I would know about it if she has. She tells me everything. Trust me, Officer-"

"Detective."

"Oh – whatever! She's only 18-years-old and she's been up all night in tears at what has happened to her. She's traumatised. She's not going to be giving any useful evidence to you right now. I should know! I worked as a secretary for-"

Dawson rolls his eyes again and looks in through the tiny window on the door of Interview Room 2. Emily's staring at her hands again, stretched over the table. Her eyes are still tear-filled and her lip is trembling. He imagines one of his own daughters in a similar situation and his heart bleeds. But she's a massive contribution to evidence in convicting Kitson, he thinks to himself, chewing his lip.

"-and they never, ever locked up a victim, it's barbaric, it's-"

"Okay, Mrs Long. Thank you. Look, I don't think you truly realise how crucial a puzzle piece your daughter is in this jigsaw. I appreciate she's going through a very hard time and it must be stressful. So, I'm going to ask you to take her home. Get her relaxed and washed. But 9am tomorrow morning, I want her back in this interview room, you hear me? And not a minute later!"

"Thank you, Detective."

Half an hour later, Dawson glances into Interview Room 1's square window. There he is. James Kingston.

"One of these boys has something to do with what's going on in this town," Dawson says, more to himself than anyone else. "And I'm determined to get to the bottom of it."

Entering Interview Room 2, he's met with a beautiful blonde girl. She smiles at him with sad eyes as he sits down and introduces McNally and himself. He goes over the procedures and what's expected. She smiles and nods to every question thrown her way.

"So, shall we begin?" McNally smiles at her and lifts up his sheets of paper. "Okay, Miss Patterson, can you start by telling us what happened last night?"

The girl tilts her head to the side and her eyes light up.

"What would you like to know?"

"Well, Miss Patterson... Is it okay if we call you Stacey?"

CHAPTER 29:

Roberta stands outside Rong Valley's Police Station waiting for any kind of information. The weather is starting to get cold and she's shivering in her thin summer shirt. A few other members of the local press have shown up, more appropriately dressed than herself, but she thanks her lucky stars that there's still no sign of that bitch, Claire. She fetches out her trusty Blackberry, clicks open her e-mails and re-reads the press release again and again. No hint to who has been arrested. Were they working together? This could be an interesting turn of events if *'The Rong Valley Teen Killer'* was, in fact, a duo stalking our streets. Her fourth re-read is interrupted by the office calling.

"Budds?"

"Roberta, how's it going at the station?"

"Still nothing. Not so much as an officer popping out for his lunch."

"Fine, well I've texted Dawson asking him to let me know as soon as anything is being made public. But for now, I need you to get down to Gemma Norris' house. She saw the news this morning and phoned in looking to speak to you."

"Me?"

"Yeah, am I right in saying you were door-stepping at her house last week?"

"Er... Yes, sir. But I-"

143

"Don't even think about making excuses. Of course I was going to find out. But you've wriggled out of my net this time, *again*. Now go and get me my exclusive!"

CHAPTER 30:

How the fuck did I end up here? I'm physically shaking as Dawson and some new detective, he introduces himself as DS McNally, I recognise him from off the telly, sit down opposite me. This room is like a cooker. And this itchy pyjama-like tracksuit doesn't help. I loosen the collar to let a bit of air in, fanning myself. I'm getting so claustrophobic.

"Not comfortable, James?" McNally perks his head to the side.

"Not very," I give an uneasy laugh, much to the annoyance of Dawson.

"Well, if you're open and honest with us, hopefully you won't be in here for much longer, understand?"

I nod and they read me the same old shit you hear on cop shows, only this time it's real life.

"So, James," Dawson leans back in his chair as far as he can go, which, in this stuffy room and with his giant belly, isn't very far at all. "No lawyer?"

"No, I don't think I need one."

"Well, you didn't have one the past few times we've met. And things didn't work out very well then, now did they?"

"No, but I'm ready to tell the truth this time."

Dawson raises his eyebrows and nods.

"Nice to start."

"Look, I haven't been lying about my whereabouts the night Derek was killed, or when Gemma was attacked. I genuinely was in bed and I know that that doesn't substitute for an alibi."

"But the Saturday morning, when Stephen was attacked?"

"Yes, I *was* lying."

The tension in the room increases significantly, if that's even possible.

"Look, it's not bad. Well... It is bad. But not as bad as you think. I've just been lying to protect myself. And someone else, in a way. The times you asked me before, we were in front of Dean... Mr Deans. I just didn't want to speak in front of him."

"So why didn't you ask for him to leave the room?"

"He'd know something was up."

"Then why didn't you contact me after, or outside of school?"

"'cause I've been lying to myself, okay?"

Dawson and McNally stare at me, eyes cold and lips bitten. Dawson nods for me to continue.

"Whatever I say in here, it stays in here, right?"

Dawson snorts softly.

"On the contrary, Mr Kingston, no. This isn't confession. As you well know, we're recording this entire-"

"Yes, I know that. But I mean, it won't go out in the press? My parents won't find out?"

"Well, I guess it all depends on how *bad* the situation is, I'm afraid. If it's as interesting as I think it is, I'm sure it *will* be leaked to the press. Through no fault of our own. They have a way of sniffing things out. But if you're innocent, which you claim, then I don't see how it has anything to do with our investigation. And as for your parents, you're a 19-year-old man now, James. Mummy and Daddy aren't here to hold your hand. We're under no obligation to tell them anything."

I hold my breath and close my eyes. It's now or never.

"Okay. Well... That night when I was out with Teddy and all his flatmates... I've been giving false alibis and lying about my whereabouts because... Well... I went home with another girl."

I exhale loudly. It feels as though a huge load is lifted from my shoulders. I suddenly feel so much better coming out in the open. I peep one eye open. Dawson looks unimpressed.

"And this girl is...?"

"Her name's Lydia. Lydia Holmes. She lives in an apartment on Promised Hill."

Dawson's face physically grimaces.

"And why didn't you tell me this before?"

"I'm ashamed. I haven't told anybody this. Ever! You're the first. I'm disgusted with myself. I cheat on my girlfriend with Lydia. I have been for over a year."

The two detectives haven't changed their facial expressions since I told them my biggest secret. After a few moments of silence, McNally turns to Dawson with raised brows.

"Fine, James. I hope you know that we *will* be contacting Miss Holmes to clarify that she was with you that night?"

"I'm not happy with it, but if it gets me out of here, I'll have to grin and bear it."

"But if I find out you're lying to me *again*," Dawson spits at me through gritted teeth, finger pointing directly at me. And with that, they both stop the recording and walk out of the room without a single look back.

Oh, no. What have I done now?

CHAPTER 31:

"So, what do you think, boss?"

McNally bites into his tuna sandwich and spills half the contents onto the canteen table. Dawson turns his nose up as McNally picks the pieces up and stuffs them back between his bread.

"I don't know, McNally. Kitson has the correct profile. Previous convictions. Aggressive, with a history of violence. ASBOs. Lives on Promised Hill, the fish tank of all crime in this town. He has a motive for murdering Derek French. But what about the other two victims? He's a bad egg, you can just tell. Kingston, on the other hand, has lied to me day in and day out since the start of this investigation. Why would you not admit to shagging some girl from Promised Hill when questioned in a very high-profile investigation? I know she's more than likely not got a lot going for her. Heck, I'd probably never admit to banging someone from up there, but if it saved my skin?"

"And he has no motive," McNally says, bits of tuna flying from his mouth.

"That we know of," Dawson rubs his chin and taps his unopened lunch box.

"So, where do we go from here?"

"Well, Emily's not coming back until tomorrow morning, so I say we give Kitson a night in the cells to stew over. Maybe he'll be a bit more cooperative in the morning. As for Kingston, I'd say we go and give his little girlfriend a visit."

"Who? Stacey Patterson? We just sent her home."

"No, McNally," Dawson stands up and tosses his uneaten lunch in the bin. "His other one."

Lydia Holmes opens the graffitied door of flat 8F after the third knock.

"Miss Holmes?"

"Yeah, who's asking?" she chews gum and stares up at the detectives with a bored face. Her stained white vest and denim three quarter length shorts barely take the attention away from her spiked Mohawk, which doesn't so much as reach the knot on the detective's ties. Now I know why he wouldn't admit to sleeping with her, Dawson thinks to himself.

"My name is Detective Inspector Donald Dawson. This is Detective Sargent Liam McNally. We would like to ask you a few questions. May we come in?"

Upon realising who her guests were, and staring at their badges, Lydia's mouth flops open, the gum falling to their feet.

"Who is it?" a voice shouts from inside the flat.

"Two seconds," Lydia bends her neck behind the wood and screams back. She steps over the threshold and closes the door behind her.

"What's this about? Am I in trouble?"

"No, Miss Holmes," McNally chuckles. "We'd just like t-"

"Well then I'd appreciate it if you'd get away from my flat. I'm sure you know that your crowd aren't exactly welcome around these parts. Now if that's all-"

Dawson's patience is wearing thin on this investigation.

"We're here to discuss your relationship with James Kingston."

Lydia stares at Dawson, before blinking furiously.

"Er... I have no idea what you're talking about."

"Mr Kingston said he spent the night here, at your flat, on the night of Saturday Septem-"

"Look, I have no idea who you're talking about. I have never heard of this... Jamie Knighton in my life. Now if that's all."

She opens the door and slams it behind her. The sound of several locks can be heard sliding into place from behind it. Dawson and McNally both look at each other and sigh. Dawson raises his hands to knock on the door again, but stops suddenly.

"Did you hear that?"

They listen attentively, but all that can be heard is the muffled sounds of the flats surrounding them.

"Psssst."

There it is again. Both officers turn to their left to see an old man peeking out of the door of 8E. They shift towards him suspiciously.

"Sir, have you got something-"

The old man waves his hands and hushes him.

"I'll tell you what I know, but come in here, I don't want any of the neighbours spotting you."

Both officers share a concerned glance before stepping into the flat of the old man, who looks up and down the corridor before snapping the door shut behind him.

CHAPTER 32:

Roberta is taken aback by the marble staircase that welcomes her as soon as she enters the huge home of the Norris family. She whistles and purses her lips, gazing around at the design of the downstairs hallway. She knew the homes around this part of town were fancy, but she never guessed that they'd reach this level of grandeur. She's shown through to the black sparkly kitchen by the elderly man who shut the door in her face last week, now introduced as Gemma's grandfather. Through the kitchen and into an open conservatory, and sitting on the rich cream 'L' shaped sofa is Gemma. Looking at her there in her thick white dressing gown, you would never think this girl had went through a traumatic time. Except her eyes. Her eyes circulate the room constantly, even when Roberta introduces herself and sits down on the giant foot stool facing her, which is comfier than her own sofa at home.

"Now, Gemma. It's nice to finally meet you. May I ask what changed your mind in agreeing to talk to me?"

Gemma's eyes rest on her father and mother, sitting across the room in a love-seat. Her dad nods his approval with a warm smile.

"Erm… Well, I didn't want my name in the papers. It's awful. Everyone knowing what I went through. But Daddy convinced me that it's a good thing. That I'm brave and by talking, I can help get this man behind bars and protect other girls from similar situations."

"That's a very brave thing to do, Gemma. I completely agree with your dad."

Roberta beams a smile towards Mr Norris.

"And also he wants me to talk about-"

Gemma's stopped by a quick '*ssh*' from her father. "Not yet dear."

Roberta looks from father to daughter and then shakes off the interruption.

"Okay, well if you'd like to start from the beginning, if you don't mind."

She brings out her reporter's pad, flicking through page after page. She really needs to get a new one, even though this one hasn't even celebrated its week-old birthday yet. Finally, finding an empty page close to the back, she hovers her pen over the crumpled sheet.

Gemma shrugs.

"I was at Sally's house. We were just messing around on Facebook and that. Then I walked home. That's when it happened."

"What time was this around?"

"About half one or twoish."

"Excuse me for asking, but is that not a little late for a young girl like yourself to be walking around at night by herself? Especially through Promised Hill?"

"That's what we keep telling her," her dad nods.

"Yeah? Well I wouldn't have had to walk home by myself, would I? If we hadn't fallen out?"

"I didn't fall out with you, sweetie. You were being unreasonable."

"All I wanted was some money to go to the shops."

"You were at the shops the day before and spent a fortune in Topshop when I asked you to get school supplies."

"I got them black boots, didn't I?"

"That were not suitable for school, now stop embarrassing us and continue with the story."

Gemma crosses her arms and stares out of the window into the well-trimmed garden outside. Her mum unravels herself from her husband's embrace, apologises to Roberta and sinks down beside her daughter. After some muffled whispers that Roberta struggles to hear, the interview resumes.

"I was walking down David's Street and heard a noise. Then, someone came out of the trees and pushed me to the ground, before digging his knife into me. Doctors say if one of the wounds was a few inches either side, I could've died. Luckily I didn't pass out, or I might've. I rang the ambulance right away and they helped me."

Roberta scribbles her shorthand furiously on her pad.

"And your attacker? Sorry to bring it up, but do you remember anything? It's been a while now, has any memories came back?"

Gemma leans her head back and stares at the pristine white ceiling.

"Not really. Like I've said, I didn't see his face. I remember his breathing. Really raspy and heavy. And a black hoody. And black shoes."

"Do you remember what type?"

"Like Converse?"

"Converse?"

"No, like them. They didn't have the logo or anything. Probably a cheap pair you'd buy somewhere for a few quid. Nothing like the real things."

As Roberta continues to write in her notepad, Gemma shifts about on her seat uncomfortably.

"I walked past a man with a similar hoody and shoes sitting on a bench just up the street. I have a feeling that's him. He followed me from there. If only I'd have gone the long way around, or just saw him as suspicious. I – I..."

She starts to sob, but as Roberta looks up, she blows out and composes herself, fanning her eyes.

"I'm being silly. I got it easy. I'm far better off than Derek."

Roberta cocks her head to the side.

"You speak about Derek like you knew him."

"I do. Well... I did. Sally used to go out with him. He seemed nice enough. Didn't really speak to him. Different friend groups, you know?"

"And Stephen?"

She shrugs.

"Know his face from the corridors."

Roberta gazes into Gemma's eyes a while longer.

"Gemma, why do you think this man had an interest in you? In Stephen? In Derek? Are you all linked somehow?"

She shrugs again.

"Same school, that's about it. Isn't that the police's job to find out?"

Roberta nods admittedly.

"What would you like to say to other kids your age, to protect them on the streets?"

Gemma glances at her dad again.

"I thought he has been arrested."

Roberta closes her notepad quietly.

"Well, there *are* two people in for questioning. But that doesn't mean-"

"We all know that helping police with their inquiries means that they've been arrested," Gemma's dad booms from across the room. "Could you give us more information? The police are giving us diddly-squat!"

"I'm sorry, Mr Norris, but at this stage in the investigation I'm afraid you know just as much as I do. I've just come here from the station. I left because they're keeping everything hush hush. I genuinely wish I could tell you, but I'm just as in the dark as yourselves."

Mr Norris looks out of the window, biting his lip and shaking his head.

"Well, if that's everything, I better be off."

"No, wait. Tell her, sweetheart."

Roberta looks at Gemma again, smiling sweetly.

"We'd like to make an appeal to people."

"Yeah, that's what this story is. But with the very little details you've given, we doubt anyone-"

"No, not about the attacker. We'd like to ask for money. It's for a business called Pink Stripes Charity. They look after young girls who have been the victims of abuse. They were introduced to me through the police. I didn't want anything to do with them at first. But a member came to the house and really helped me through everything."

Roberta smiles and nods.

"That's very nice. I will-"

"Yes," Mr Norris takes over. "We gave them a grand there a few days ago as a thank you and to help keep their services active for other young girls going through similar circumstances."

"Oh, well... I'll make sure to plug their website at the end of the story and state that they accept donations. Now if you don't mind-"

Roberta stands to leave and Mr Norris joins her on his feet.

"Thanks again, Roberta," Mr Norris places his hand on her lower back and starts escorting her out of the room, whilst Mrs Norris plays with Gemma's hair and reassures her how well she had done.

"And don't forget to include that we contributed a grand to the cause. Here's my card if you need any more quotes or information."

As the journalist turns the corner and out of the kitchen, she isn't quite out of ear shot from Gemma, who asks her hushing mother, "Will Daddy buy me that new car now?"

Roberta fakes a smile as Mr Norris waves her goodbye at the door. As she makes her way down the drive towards her car, suddenly looking considerably tackier behind the likes of the Norris' Mercedes and BMW, she shakes her head at the bemusement of the family. She starts her engine and reverses out of the drive.

"Nothing but an egotistic, attention seeking asshole with a spoilt brat of a daughter."

Her blood is boiling as she starts her journey back to the office.

CHAPTER 33:

Dawson can't help but overcome the sensation to gag at the smell of the old man's flat. Burnt microwave cooking and pipe smoke mixed with the strong scent of damp clings to the yellowing walls and consumes everything else in the dark studio.

"Please, sit, sit," the elderly man says whilst boiling the kettle.

"Where?" Dawson mouths to McNally, arms outstretched. McNally barely conceals his snort of laughter as he scrunches down on to newspapers covering the old ripped leather sofa. Dawson takes a seat beside him and gazes around the pathetic studio flat. He should feel a pang of guilt looking at how this old man lives, but he believes that the man has done something in his life to end up here. Whether he be an alcoholic, a junkie or on benefits because he's too lazy to work. The man comes down with two shaky cups of tea. Dawson raises his top lip with disgust at the dirt of the cup. Is that mould growing on the rim? Dawson smiles and places his cup on the stained carpet.

"So, Mr...?"

"Heggarty. Tobias Heggarty."

"Mr Heggarty, you said you'd tell us everything you know about Miss Holmes next door?"

"Ssssh," Tobias exclaims, fingers to his lips. He shuffles over to the far corner and presses his ear to the wall.

Dawson and McNally share a glance and then return their attention to Tobias. After a few moments, Tobias resumes his place in the armchair beside the battered bulky TV.

"Thin walls," he whispers. "But I can hear music playing, so we should be okay."

He gazes at McNally, sitting with his cup at his chest. Out of politeness, McNally takes a sip from his cup and splutters.

"Too hot."

"Would you like some milk?"

"No, no, fine. I don't like my tea too milky, I'll wait for it to cool."

Dawson can't let himself begin to think how curdled the milk would be.

"And yourself, Detective Inspector Dawson?"

Dawson stares at him. How did Tobias know his name? He must've been listening through his door.

"Not a big tea drinker, but thanks."

"I have coffee, hot chocolate, water?"

"No thanks, Mr Heggarty. I'd rather get back to the station soon, if you don't mind. We have a lot of work to do."

"I'll say. Massive investigation. I'm guessing this has got something to do with the recent attacks on youngsters?"

"I'm afraid we can't disclose a lot of information at the moment, Tobias," McNally tries to make himself comfortable in the bed of papers.

"May I ask why you were asking my neighbour about James?"

"You know him?"

"Well, I've never spoken to him, if that's what you're implying. But I know he comes over every now and then, when Lydia's girlfriend, Clara, is out."

Dawson is speechless. He knew the girl was lying about not knowing James, but he never thought for a second that James was telling the truth.

"You were asking Lydia if James was over on a certain Saturday. The Saturday that that Stephen Begley boy got attacked, I presume?"

"Yes," McNally spurts out before Dawson can stop him.

"Let me see here," Tobias groans as he struggles to lift himself out of his chair. As he limps over to the greying cupboards beside the TV, the elderly man passes both detectives, who wince at the smell of him. He clearly hasn't showered in days.

"Saturday the 10th, wasn't it?"

McNally gives a sideways glance at Dawson, who shrugs in surrender.

"Yes, Tobias."

Tobias shuffles around in the cupboards a while longer before bringing out a bulging writers pad. Flicking through the pages, he reaches just over half way and returns to his seat.

"Yes, he was there that morning, or the Friday night, if you prefer."

"I'm sorry, Mr Heggarty," Dawson's curiosity has gotten the better of him. "But what, may I ask, is that?"

"What? *This*?" Tobias raises the notepad in the air as if it were the most natural thing in the world. "Well, it gets very lonely around these parts, you see Detective. I have no family or friends and am pretty much left to myself. A few years back, the girl who lived in 8B, she's moved out now, had her home burgled. Now it just so happens that she worked lates in... Er... the bar."

Dawson nods politely, knowing full well that this meant she was either a hooker or a stripper.

"But no-one knew of her work schedule except her manager, who she was seeing for a while. I saw them together. Quite a cute couple, you know, if you're into the tattoos and the ear piercings and stretching to make them look like onion rings."

McNally snorts from laughter again, both Dawson and Tobias gazing at him until he apologises.

"Well anyway, I'd heard the two rowing for a few weeks. He went storming out one evening. Just so happens that I was still up when she left for work later that same night. I don't get a lot of sleep, you know? Not since..."

He smiles and shakes his head.

"Not important. Well, about a half hour later I saw him return to the property. He left a few minutes later with her TV and a few other items. Now, I knew that they'd been seeing each other, so I just thought they'd broken up and he'd come to reclaim his belongs. But, when she got back the next morning she was hysterical. Screaming that the flat had been trashed and she'd been burgled. Wanted to know if any of us had seen anything. Of course, I was able to confirm that I *had* seen him. Long story short, she loved me for it and I think she got some of her possessions back.

"Since then, I've started a sort of diary of what goes on. As you well know, this neighbourhood is no walk in the park. I won't bother you with the details of what this building sees every day, but in terms of what goes on on this floor, and out on the street from the window

162

there," he points towards the filthy sliding doors to the balcony, overlooking the street at the front entrance of the flats.

"Anything out of the ordinary that goes on, I document it. Not a lot of people ask about it, but if I can help in anyway, then I feel like I've accomplished something. You never know when it could come in handy. And it looks like it has worked. I'm guessing that poor James is looking for an alibi?"

"Again, we can't discuss anything-"

"Surely, I understand. Well here it is. All in writing."

Tobias hands over the grimy pad and Dawson and McNally lean their heads together to read. With the weak lighting and the handwriting almost as untidy as this flat, it's hard to make out, but after a few seconds of struggling, they find what they're looking for.

'2:46am. James stumbles up the stairs and starts hammering on Lydia's door. She's still not back from her night out. He slumps down outside her door and sits on his phone.

'3:04am. Lydia appears and lets James in. They've started kissing before the door is even closed. Must be drunker than other nights.'

Dawson shakes his head in disbelief. Surely enough, a few lines down shows him leaving the next morning. He starts flicking through the pad, looking at previous dates, skimming for James' name. And there it is. August 28th. August 14th. July 19th. It's all here.

"Mr Heggarty, you don't mind if we take this to the office and make copies for evidence?"

"Be my guest, anything to protect someone who is innocent."

"I don't believe it."

Dawson is back in the studio pondering over the tape of James at The Fork and Spoons Bar. He watches him look at his phone and leave the bar at 2:32am. According to Google Maps, it would take less than ten minutes to drive from the bar to Lydia's flat on Promised Hill. That weird old man was able to give him a solid alibi, even if Lydia wasn't. He leaves the studio and starts towards his office, deep in thought.

"Sir?"

He almost walks straight past McNally without acknowledgement.

"Can I have a word?"

Gathered in Dawson's office, McNally's latest research is laid out on Dawson's desk.

"So I did a background check on Tobias. Nothing came up on our system. I did a bit of research and found out he's formerly known as George Reid, a convicted paedophile from Bolton. Almost fifty years ago, he claimed his innocence in not knowing the age of a 14-year-old boy when he performed oral sex on him. He pleaded guilty in court to receive a minor sentence, but because he was the grounds keeper at the local school, he got *a lot* of backlash in the press. When he left prison, he received a new identity and was situated just south of Leeds. But the lads that were after him found him and beat him to a pulp. Nearly killed him. He moved here and has been living on Promised Hill ever since."

Dawson looks at the pictures and documents in front of him, shaking his head.

"Does this make him an unreliable witness?"

"Unfortunately not, McNally."

"Sir?"

"We can't hold someone accountable for something they did in another lifetime. Discharge the boy."

"Are you sure?"

"No, I'm not, if truth be told. But there's nothing else we can do except keep an eye on him. Let's just hope that we get better results tomorrow with Kitson."

CHAPTER 34:

Line 2 flashes green at Rong Valley Herald's news desk.

"Roberta Mills."

"Hi, Roberta. It's Gareth Norris here."

It takes all of Roberta's energy to not put down the phone. She holds it out in front of her and blows a raspberry in disgust.

"How can I help you?"

"I'm just sitting here with this morning's paper in front of me. But there's only a tiny segment on Gemma's interview, with a short line about the charity. I'm just wondering what went wrong? I e-mailed you a lot of information and pictures. It looks nothing like the spread that the Begley kid got a few weeks back."

"Well, Stephen Begley gave me his interview very shortly after his attack. Your daughter's story was just a refresher. To get people thinking again."

"But you didn't even include that we contributed the thousand pounds to the charity."

Roberta bites her tongue and grips the phone tight.

"I'm sorry?"

"I just feel like it would help people to contribute if they knew we were."

"I apologise, Mr Norris, but I work on the crime desk here at the Herald. If you are interested in soft news, I can transfer you to one of my colleagues, or you could get in touch with the media team at the local university. I'm afraid I have to go now, big stories coming up, good day!"

And with that, Roberta slams the phone down, a little too forceful as several of the surrounding journalists give her a disapproving look. Roberta can't help it.

"Stuck up prick," she hisses to herself as she refreshes her Twitter notifications.

"Trouble, Roberta?"

Roberta puts on her best fake smile and swivels her chair around.

"Oh nothing, Budds."

"Who was it?"

"Just Gemma Norris' dad. He was looking for me to do a story on a charity that has helped Gemma. He's donated a thousand pounds."

"Just looking for a bit of publicity then?"

"Yes, sir."

He tuts and sits down on the corner of her desk.

"I've got word back from Dawson, one of the boys that was taken in for questioning was allowed to go home last night."

"What? What about the second?"

"They're speaking to him this morning. Apparently a mouthy little shit, so they kept him in overnight."

"But they don't have long now before they have to either charge him or let him go."

"I know. Waiting for a witness to come in first, apparently, and give a bit of evidence against him. And Dawson isn't entirely sure on either of them, to be honest. It seems they're clutching at straws over there."

He groans as he slides off the desk and hobbles over to his office. Roberta taps her pen off her cheek repeatedly, deep in thought. Her phone vibrates and she grabs for it.

'No, I don't know anything. Stop asking and leave me alone!!!!'

"Still no help," Roberta sighs.

CHAPTER 35:

As I reach over to switch my alarm off, the depression hits me again. I was almost fucking arrested. I spent my Saturday in a cell and getting interviewed by the police. I'm so grateful I got let out just before dark, or I might've had to spend the night in there. As I get up and get ready for work, Mum knocks on my door and loiters in the hallway.

"I still don't feel up to talking about it, Mum."

To be honest, I have no idea what to say.

"Just tell me everything is okay, James? We're worried sick. I didn't get a wink of sleep last night."

You and me both.

"Everything's fine, Mum. Just a mix up. So much has been going on lately. I told them I was somewhere when I thought I was. Turns out I was wrong. That's why they let me go."

Oh no, she's crying again. My heart aches as I go over and hug her. There's nothing worse than being the reason your own mother is crying.

"Has it got to do with these attacks?"

"Yeah, I told you they've been interviewing everyone in my school. I didn't have an alibi and accidently lied to them, so I was public enemy number one. And look, they've arrested someone else. I bet it's him, Mum. I just know it. I have to get ready for work." I pull away and make my way over to the wardrobe.

"It was Stacey."

I stop and turn around.

"What?"

"She came over last night asking what happened. We didn't tell her. I'm guessing you didn't, considering you didn't have your phone. And no one else knows. So how would she have known?"

My blood starts to boil.

"What did you tell her?"

"Just that we hadn't heard from you. We were about to ask her how she found out, but she went running off, clearly upset."

I pick up my phone from the bedside locker and search for her number.

"James, don't."

Too late.

"Oh, so now you decide to speak to me?"

She answers, clearly eating something.

"Oh, I think you know why I couldn't ring you sooner."

"Because you were huffing. Look, I think we should talk about Friday night."

"We should."

There's an uncomfortable silence on the line. Mum is cemented to my door frame, listening in.

"What's wrong with you?"

"Nothing."

"Why are you acting so weird?"

"I could ask you the same thing."

"Look, James. I have no idea what's wrong with you, but I did nothing wrong on Frida-"

"You really are an attention seeking bitch, you know that?"

Silence again.

"What are you talki-"

"Have a nice chat with the police yesterday, did you?"

I can't see her face, but I know what her reaction will be like.

"Why would I phone the police? Because you attacked me?"

"I never said you phoned them. And how the fuck did I attack you?" I start to scream, trembling.

"James, please, calm down," Mum comes over and starts trying to pry the phone from my hand.

"I just had to spend the better part of my Saturday in a jail cell, Stacey. All because of you."

"I have no idea what you're talking about."

"Don't play dumb with me, you conniving cunt!"

Mum gasps.

"James, I don't like the way you're speaking to me."

"Yeah? Well I don't like the way my girlfriend starts a row with me, starts hitting me and then goes crying to the police the next day. You're a fucking mess. We're done!"

I hang up the phone, switch it off and throw it on the bed.

"James you can't go to work like this."

"I'm fine!"

CHAPTER 36:

"Now, Emily. I believe you weren't being one hundred percent honest with us yesterday, were you?"

Emily looks a lot better after getting home, showered and a good night sleep. Dawson and McNally have joined her in Interview Room 2 again.

"Yeah, sorry. My mum's very overprotective. I didn't want her finding out some of the stuff that has been going on."

"Like?"

Emily shifts uncomfortably and gazes into the contents of the untouched mug in her hands.

"Like what happened on Friday night."

"Go on."

"I told Johnny I didn't want to be in a relationship with him. That I wanted to see other people. I was with Derek for over a year and I didn't want his death to be the milestone for the start of a relationship between me and Johnny. I'm not ready for that. It's too raw."

"And he didn't take it well?"

"It was when we were fighting. We both had too much to drink. But I didn't deserve that."

She starts crying, wiping the running mascara from her cheek.

"Of course you didn't," McNally chips in, patting her hand. "So, how long was this... Fling going on for?"

"Since April. We were flirting for weeks in Geography. Then on Facebook. Then he somehow got my number. We hooked up at Louise McCray's Easter party."

"And there was a fight?" Dawson interjects.

"Yeah," she nods. "We were both quite drunk and, somehow, started kissing. Derek seen and he wasn't happy. They both got into a bit of a scrap, then Derek left. We ended up sleeping together that night in Louise's mum and dad's bed. We've been meeting up in private since then."

"So, why did you lie about seeing him?"

Emily shrugs.

"Shame? Guilt? Obviously I haven't been a very nice person, and I feel worse now that Derek's dead. Johnny became obsessed with me. Used to wait for me outside my classes. He knew my timetable better than I did. Texted me all the time. Begging for me to break up with Derek. Sending me pictures of himself."

A slight blush rises in her cheeks.

"Nude pictures."

"He texted you that night, didn't he?" Dawson says, keen to change the subject. "Kitson?"

Emily nods as her eyes glaze over, the memory playing in her head.

"Yeah. Derek and I were meeting up in the park. My bedroom overlooks the child's play part. But Johnny kept texting me. Asking me to come around to his. I think he was drunk. He kept sending pictures and I was afraid of Derek seeing, so I left my phone in my room. I can

173

get through to the park from a broken panel in my fence. Derek and I had sex, but I knew something was wrong. I had a funny feeling. Like we were being watched. As soon as we were done, he wanted to go home right away. I remember being upset. I felt used. I went back and texted Johnny, but he didn't respond until morning. Claimed he'd fallen asleep. If only I hadn't have let Derek walk off by himself. I shouldn't have even met up with him at that time of night. I just... I just..."

She bursts into fresh tears and McNally soothes her.

"Emily, do you think Kitson is capable of killing Derek?" Dawson asks.

Emily nods.

"He's always been in trouble at school for fighting. Him and his friends like to attack animals. One time, when I was hanging around that corner with them, they chased a poor dog. Saying they were going to tie it to a firework and light it. I was disgusted. I cried myself to sleep that night," she continues to sob. "How did I become involved with someone like this?"

"Do you know if he had any sort of a grudge on Gemma Norris? Or Stephen Begley? Any beef at school or on social media?"

She shakes her head.

"I barely knew them, but he never mentioned them. I'd say he *would* attack them though. Whether he had a reason or not. He's just a horrible, horrible person."

Dawson nods at McNally.

"Thanks, Miss Long. We appreciate your help. You're free to go."

"Okay, okay, I admit it."

After a long few hours, Dawson nearly sighs in exhaustion.

"I were badgering Emily. I think I love her, alright? Is that what you want to hear? I don't give a fuck about other girls, but I want to see her all the time. I never feel like this, okay? It's new to me. But I swear, I never touched Derek. Except that one time at Louise's party. I might've gave him a shove back, but he got the better of me that night. Ask anyone that was there. I got a right batterin'. I swear I never touched him. Or Stephen. Or the girl. You've got to believe me?"

Not exactly what Dawson had been hoping for. He sucks his teeth in frustration as he stares at Kitson a while longer. It took long enough, but they finally broke him. This sweaty mess of a kid in front of them is not the tough scum from Promised Hill any longer. But have they got all they want from him?

"Johnny, you have no alibi for that night," McNally shakes his head. "And you've got to admit that the motive and evidence is alarming. Even texting Lydia saying you wished him dead-"

"It didn't mean I were gonna do nout," Kitson looks like he's near tears. "Just drunk and I regret it now. I really do. I pushed her away and now look at the shape I'm in. In jail for fuck sake when I done nout wrong."

"Okay, look Johnny. We don't believe you," Dawson lays both hands on the table, a bored look on his face. "We just can't-"

"Sorry to interrupt."

The party of three look up towards the crack in the door of Interview Room 1. A sheepish looking policewoman peers her head into the stuffy room.

"DI Dawson. DS McNally. We need you to terminate the interview and step outside. It's urgent."

CHAPTER 37:

Bastard!

The stupid box won't get into the bailer. I look around at the door, making sure no one's coming down the aisle. Although every health and safety rule in the book would scream at me not to, I climb feet first in and jump up and down until the Baby Born pram sinks into the teeth of the old rusty green machine.

"Thank God for that," I wipe sweat from my brow before jumping out and pressing the big yellow start button.

"Delivery came yet?" Ross pokes his head through the door. A few seconds earlier and I could've been fired.

"Nah," I sigh, feeling the vibrations of the machine through my pressing finger ricochet around my body as if I'm a human blender.

"They'd need to bloody hurry up!" he storms out.

Like it's my fault? Dick.

I shake my head. They *would* need to hurry up. Shop closes at six. Not really in the mood to be waiting around until God knows when. Almost as if on cue, the shutters give a crash. Finally, I think, as I hop down the steps towards the loading bay.

Shit, the keys! I run back into the stockroom and shout for Ross, but he's nowhere to be seen.

"I'll do it myself then," I whisper exasperated, grabbing the keys from the hook.

Out in the loading bay, I make my way to the switch, but stop abruptly when I casually glance at the TV screen on the wall. I expected to be greeted with high-vis vests and a few cages full of toys and toasters from the CCTV outside. But instead, I see a figure pressed against the shutters. What's this asshole doing? Probably some drunk trying to make his way back to the flats on Benjamin Street. I walk over to the shutter to knock and tell him to move on, but almost as if he can read my mind, he bangs the shutter again, making me jump. Grunting in disgust, I continue forward, annoyed that he startled me. But another crash greets me. And a faint cry. What the hell is he up to? I take a few steps back to glance up at the screen again and gasp. The figure has turned around and I see that he has his fist deep in a girl's stomach. The picture is pixilated but I can tell that she's bleeding.

Oh fuck, it's him!

"Oi!"

I thunder across to the switch and scramble for the keys.

Fuck! I've dropped them.

Which bloody key is it again? I make a few futile attempts before the shutter zooms into life, lifting itself up and letting the light from the alley outside flood across the loading bay. But there's a huge dark patch of blood swimming into view as well.

Holy shit!

When the shutter is at stomach height, I let go and duck down under it. On the ground is a dark-haired girl, her leather jacket covering what, moments ago, was a frilly white top. Now it's spoiled with blood. I scramble over to her and press my hand against her wound.

"Where is he?"

As I look into her face I gasp again. Morgan! Teddy's sister. She just stares at my question, panting and crying.

"Look, Morgan, it's going to be okay, alright? Ross! Help!"

I look behind me at the empty loading bay echoing my cries. As I turn back around to Morgan, I could swear I saw an image of a figure disappearing around the corner by the back of the Greggs.

CHAPTER 38:

"Why am I not surprised to see you here, Kingston?" Dawson sighs and looks disapprovingly at James.

"I swear I've had nothing to do with it. Why would I call for help? I've been in work since noon."

James is inconsolable as Dawson and McNally fight to calm him down. He's manically shaking and walking back and forth, looking ridiculous in the thick woollen blanket from the paramedics draped over his shoulders.

"I can vouch for that," Ross nods as his eyes follow James from left to right.

"And you know her?"

"Yeah, Morgan," James stops and stares at Dawson with mad eyes. "She's my best mate's sister."

"And let me guess. A student at Rong Valley High?"

"No, actually, she isn't. She goes to the all-girl Catholic school up on Evergreen."

This does change things. Dawson bites the inside of his mouth as he gazes around at the carnage on the side street. The area has been cordoned off with no one getting in or out. About half a dozen shoppers are complaining to the uniforms saying that they've got places to go. People to see. Parking to pay. Some shop owners have also vacated their stores, asking police when they can close up. All of them are getting questioned and statements will be submitted, but by the looks of things, nobody except Morgan and Kingston saw anything. The people here were just passing through when the police and paramedics arrived, or were trying to help Morgan. This is a quiet side street on the edge of the town centre. Only a handful of delivery drivers for the surrounding shops drive down here. And even fewer people take short cuts through here into town. There's a large white tent shielding the scene from the onlookers. Dawson gazes at the fresh pool of blood and wished that this Morgan girl was awake when they got here. If she knows James as well as he says, then maybe she'll give some answers. Then he spots the white CCTV camera above the shutters and thanks God that the red LED light is still illuminating.

"Ross, isn't it?"

"Yes, sir."

"Do I understand that that security camera belongs to you?"

"Yes, sir, it does. We get all sorts coming in on our deliveries. Washing machines. iPads. Laptops. You name it. All kinds of goods. We had a bloke a few years ago that thought it would be a good idea to get his mate to come and park his van over there," he points at the corner of the street, just shy of the delivery door to Marks and Spencers.

"Long story short, come delivery time, whenever the driver's back was turned, his mate took a lucky dip. Went on for months, we reckon, until a lady passing by saw them. Reported it straight to me. Needless to say, the bloke was fired and we fitted that camera days later. Reckon he stole a good few grands worth."

"And is it still working? I'm judging by the red light."

"Oh yeah, you bet. The big boss was fuming when all that happened. We've been putting a fresh tape in every week since."

"And you could submit it for evidence?"

"I'm sure I can."

Ross trudges off up the ramp to the main stockroom, mumbling about how in his day nothing was worth more than a few quid.

CHAPTER 39:

I don't breathe until I'm finally on my bed. It feels like my lungs are filled with thousands of tiny pieces of glass. I'm getting too clumsy. That was far too close. But I couldn't help it, the fucking bitch. At least it was a bit deserted. No one else was there when I fled. But out there on a street in the middle of town? I just saw red. All aspects of precaution left me. And the shop worker was so close to catching me. If he had have been a good runner, he might've caught up with me. And where would I be now? Rotting in some cell somewhere. He must've stayed to console that slut.

Luckily, the black of my hoody hid most of the blood, once I slipped my hands and knife inside my sleeves. Some people gave me funny looks as I sprinted past, but I think it's just because I was in such a rush. Flying past people, pushing past them and yelling at them to get out of my way. No-one saw the blood on my clothes or hatred and guilt in my eyes. At least, I don't think so. I made straight for the park and buried both my hoody and knife by the river. I washed my hands in the water and made my way home, trying to look as casual as possible. I'll go back later tonight if I can. I definitely wasn't followed.

But for now, I wait.

My heart rate finally returns to normal and I fight for slow deep breaths, despite my throat feeling like sandpaper. I need to be more careful next time.

CHAPTER 40:

"Well, I'll be damned."

Dawson can't believe his eyes as he watches the whole charade back in Ross' pokey little office.

"Dressed all in black again," McNally comments.

Which is true. They watch as the attacker runs away as soon as the shutter starts lifting, and out comes James.

"This is a bit too coincidental."

"Sir?"

"He gets released and the next day a girl gets attacked right outside his work? He has had to have put someone up to this."

McNally narrows his eyes as he takes in this new information. He coughs and bites his lip.

"Something to say, McNally?"

"Er... I don't agree with you, sir. Sorry. He seems genuine. I thought it the first time I seen him. Did you see how panicked he was just now?"

"Yeah 'cause we caught him in the act!"

"No, we didn't. He sounded the alarm."

"Yeah, but this person is all in black. He would've known."

"Sir, I don't mean to sound disrespectful, but I think you're nit-picking. Trying to see stuff that isn't there. We never revealed to James what the attacker was wearing."

"Well I'm sure he'd know if he was the murderer."

McNally sniffs and returns his gaze at the screen, looking like he has far more to say. Dawson shakes his head and exhales.

"Well, you know what this means, don't you?"

Dawson looks straight at McNally, disappointment etched all over his face.

"What, McNally?"

"We have to let Johnny go."

As soon as he says it, Dawson's eyes close and he moans.

"We have to release him in a few hours anyway. We don't have sufficient evidence for an arrest."

"Well, we keep an eye on him. And I mean a *very* close eye. Uniforms tailing him if we have to."

Dawson and McNally stumble down the dreary corridor and out into the stockroom, ready to ascend the stairs up on to the shop floor.

"You okay, sir?"

"No, McNally. If truth be told, I'm not. We're almost a month into this investigation and have nothing to show for it. If anything, it feels like we're right back at the beginning again. Where is this going to end? Now, with this new attack, the press are going to be back beating down on us worse than before. I hope this girl pulls through, for our sake as well as her own."

CHAPTER 41:

"Why the hell are you closing so early?"

I'm being escorted out of The Old Hen, but it can't be midnight yet.

"I'm sorry, mate. It's a Sunday. You know the rules, I see you in here all the time."

Loitering around at the front door, I try to persuade the doorman to let me in for one more, but he's having none of it. Staggering across the road, I start down Chessington Street, but I know it's a lost cause. I'm met with shutter after shutter. Everywhere is closed, even in this busy part of town. I plonk myself down on the steps of the Tesco Express. I needed a drink after that incident. Dawson took a statement from me, but thankfully let me go shortly after. He didn't seem too happy about it. I think he believes it was me. Some elaborate scheme to prove my innocence. It's shook me up big time.

Lydia is still dodging my texts. I check Facebook. She was online three minutes ago. She definitely doesn't have a computer, so she's clearly on her phone. Ignoring me. I call her, but after two rings it goes straight to voicemail. She's hanging up on me intentionally. I try again and again, but it keeps happening. I almost throw my phone at the ground in frustration, but hug my knees around my body instead. What is this weird feeling I'm having towards Lydia? It can't be love. I know what love feels like. I love Stacey. Or *loved* Stacey, until she handed me over to Dawson for something I haven't done. Hard to believe she could become even more of a psycho.

I can't explain the desire I have to see Lydia though. I just want to be in her apartment, even if it is a shithole. As long as I see her. I click onto her Facebook profile picture. I could recognise her bathroom a mile off. Staring at the dirty shower in the background of the photo, I remember the time we climbed in, clothes on, and went at it. That was one of the better nights. She was very drunk. Allowed me to stay over and even cuddled into me in the middle of the night. Must've thought I was Clara. Then I start flicking through her pictures and grind my teeth. I want to see her. Now! Why won't she answer me? After the fifth time calling, my fingers scroll down to the previous caller. Twenty-six missed calls. Stacey.

Half an hour later, I'm on top of her. She catches my drunken stench, but is so happy I'm there she doesn't mind. She just moans in my ear and scrapes at my back. She's not Lydia, but she'll have to do. For now anyway. When I'm finished, I roll over on my side and wipe my brow. My stomach's turning with the alcohol and my head's starting to pound. She tries to cuddle me, but I elbow her out of the way. My mind starts to clear and I'm beginning to assess the situation. What am I doing? Hobbling around in the dark, I start looking for my clothes. I think she's trying to start a fight. I'm not paying attention. The odd hysteric whisper penetrates my brain. How dare I come over. How could I? I haven't said a word since I got here. Blah-blah-blah.

She's crying as I go to leave.

"So, this is really it?"

I totter at the door and sway slightly. Closing one eye to see better, I look at her and hiccup.

"You've got no-one to blame but yourself."

As I turn to leave, I see her reach for her pint glass of water, but her bedroom door is safely closed before it smashes into the space where I was mere seconds before.

CHAPTER 42:

"Miss Brown?"

Morgan slowly opens her eyes and, with great difficulty due to the many bandages around her waist, moves up the bed to get more comfortable. McNally sits down timidly in the green stained visitor's chair of the hospital, whilst Dawson continues to stand. She's in bad shape, he thinks to himself, but hopefully she remembers something.

"We're here to talk to you about your attack last night. Are you able to speak right now?"

"I guess," Morgan coughs as the blood seems to return to her face and cheeks.

"So, as you've probably guessed, Miss Brown. Or can I call you Morgan? Morgan – right. Well, you know we're trying to find the person responsible for the attacks on Gemma Norris, Stephen Begley and the murder of Derek French. We believe your attacker is the same person. We've viewed the tapes and by his height, build and dress sense, we are quite positive that he's the same perpetrator. Therefore, it'd be great for us to know any information which can lead to his arrest. Did you see anything?"

Tears fill Morgan's eyes as she shakes her head.

"Oh, I knew he was the same guy. I just knew it. I'm so sorry, but I didn't see anything. I don't even remember anyone following me, or knew he was behind me when it happened. I was just making my way to the bus stop when I felt someone grab me. Then it's all a blur. I barely even remember James finding me. Only through other people telling me. I'm so sorry. I want to help. I really do. But I can't."

"Would James Kingston have anything towards you? A vendetta, if you will?" Dawson's eyes narrow.

"James? No, of course not. We barely speak. Just the odd *'hiya'* when he's around ours. Oh, no. James wouldn't be like that…"

McNally reassures Morgan as Dawson marches out of the room, unable to hide the annoyance and impatience on his face. How has this person hid themselves so well?

"I just hope they're not hiding in plain sight," Dawson mutters. "Not like last time."

CHAPTER 43:

Oh my God, I shouldn't have come to school today. The bright canteen burns my eyes as I squint at the queue beginning to die down. My stomach is still turning, despite it being lunch time, but I need food in my system if I have any hope of paying even the slightest bit of attention in Maths class in twenty minutes. Picking up the plastic red tray, I fill in behind the half a dozen students still waiting. My head's splitting as I bring out my fourth bottle of water. What was I thinking drinking so much when I knew I had to come in today? I just hope that no-one notices. I texted Teddy before I called my taxi to see how Morgan is, but he hasn't replied. Probably still at the hospital. I sent her a message on Facebook to let her know I was thinking about her. I know she's alive, but that's all.

As I reach the front of the queue, I order my lasagne and turn around to trudge off to the tills. But I don't see Crystal Cummings trying to slip herself between myself and the person in front. My tray slaps off her stomach and the lasagne topples off all over her white school shirt. She screams and stands with her hands outstretched in disgust. A few kids around us begin to laugh. It spreads, causing a ripple effect of giggles until the whole room's eyes are on us.

"Oh, I – I – I'm so sorry, Crystal. I had no idea you wer-"

"You *freak*!"

Crystal starts brushing the mince and cheese off her shirt, but the tomato sauce has already begun to sink in.

"You absolutely stink of drink. It's a Monday morning you sad bastard. In Mr Deans' office having a few brandies before you come down for your lunch, were you?"

"What are y-"

"Oh, don't play innocent. We all know you're the principal's pet. Get away with ditching class, stabbing kids and even murder. And now, drinking in school."

My mouth falls open as a few kids start joining in, anonymously shouting '*yeah, murderer*' and '*go to jail where you belong*.' A half full carton of milk just narrowly misses my head.

"What? You angry that this sauce isn't blood? Better watch myself next time I'm walking around on my own, shall I?"

"Now what is all this? Crystal what has happened to your shirt?"

Mrs Merchant has come over to calm the situation down, but I'm too angry to stick around. I throw the remainder of my untouched lunch on the tiled floor and storm out of the canteen.

I'm sat in Maths class when the rest of the kids begin to flood in. Some give me the usual funny look, giving me the impression that they weren't in the canteen. But then, several come in and look my way with a smirk. Within seconds, everyone is staring at me. I ignore the whispering and giggles and stare straight ahead, waiting for Mrs Porter.

"James?"

The voice is quite timid, which makes me question who's come to slag me off now. As I turn my head, I see Andrew Daniels standing with one hand rubbing his shoulder, the other holding his bag, hanging loosely by his side.

"Mind if I sit down for a sec?"

I'm left in complete shock that I'm not quite sure what noise I make. Something between a 'yeah' and a 'uh-uh.' He sits down in the vacant chair next to me and I move my text book over, having not being used to sharing desks since the start of the year.

"Look, I just wanted to let you know that I saw what happened in the lunch hall. Crystal was trying to cut in to get another free apple pie. She pushes her luck and I see it every day. It could've happened to anyone. In regards to you being the principal's pet, I don't think there's anything wrong with that. I think it's nice. He might be an alcoholic, but-"

"Wow, hey, wait. Deans is not an alcoholic."

Andrew blushes sheepishly and leans his head in closer.

"It's okay, James. I'm in his English class and I sit right at the front. He comes in after maybe twenty minutes away and he smells like a brewery. Everyone knows it."

I blink furiously at him as my brain starts to whirl. I guess he always does disappear during class and is *always* late. But I've never actually smelt drink off him. Or have I? I went to visit him just ten minutes ago, fresh from the canteen. He'd calmed me down as I told him I wanted to drop out. That Mrs Porter had told him I was doing well and I'd be out of here soon. Andrew fidgets awkwardly before looking at the sniggering kids behind him.

"And to be honest, I know you're not a killer. I believe you didn't do all those things to them kids. You don't have it in you. I know the kids all think you have, but don't let them bother you. You're a nice person, pal. From what I've seen anyway."

I smile awkwardly, I've never taken compliments well.

"Erm… Thanks, mate. I appreciate it."

He nods and stands up abruptly as Mrs Porter comes hobbling into the room.

"Anyway, see ya."

He skims over my desk and makes towards the other side of the room, perching himself down beside Ethan Gort, who whispers something in Andrew's ear before looking over in my direction. I pretend I don't notice and stare out of the window. Well, what do you know? Maybe this school isn't filled entirely with assholes after all.

CHAPTER 44:

"Come on mate, *please*. I'm begging you."

Teddy's throwing the deflating basketball up and catching it in his hands. Letting the ball get that bit closer to his face every time.

"I'm telling you, not a hope in hell!"

He's trying to get me to go to Louise McCray's 18th birthday party tomorrow night. Although it's been a few days since Lasagne Gate, I still hear people sniggering at me in the corridors. I'm getting scrunched up pieces of papers lobbed at my head during class. I opened one of them to see a message saying, *'Die murderer scum.'* Charming. Now he really thinks he's going to convince me to spend my Saturday night at a party filled with them?

"How's Morgan?"

She's still in hospital, but from what I've heard, she's doing a lot better.

"Don't change the subject! You know she's going to be fine. Please, mate. Latonya's so fit, you have no idea."

"Latonya? Who the hell is she? I thought you were going to the party to see Teri."

"Yeah, yeah. I am. But I heard earlier from a trustworthy source that Latonya's going to be there too. You know I can't resist a girl with a nose ring. Please, mate. I don't want to go by myself. I'll look stupid going to a kid's party when I'm at uni."

"Oh, cheers mate. It'll look so much better for you to show up with me, supposed to be at uni but forced to repeat the year and is now known as the school murderer."

Teddy catches his ball and flinches slightly. He'd forgotten who he was talking to.

"I'm sorry about that, Jamie boy. But look, you and Stacey have just broken up. You know the best way to get over someone? Get under someone else. You know what I'm saying?"

I laugh and shake my head. If only he knew that I was more upset that Lydia wasn't responding to my texts than I was about the breakup. As expected, Stacey didn't take it well. She was constantly texting, calling, Whatsapping. Anything to get in contact with me. She had even come out to my house, but Mum hadn't let her through the door. Every time my phone went off, I wanted it desperately to be Lydia, only to see Stacey's name again and again. I'm scrolling through Facebook when, speak of the devil, Lydia's name appears on the home screen. She's asking if everyone is wearing costumes to this party tomorrow, and if they are, what are they wearing?

My heart skips. She's going.

A few posts ago, I seen that that kid Andrew had put up a taster of his costume. I search for his name and message him.

'Hey man, you going to that party tomorrow?'

He sees it and the icon tells me he's writing back almost immediately.

'Yeah, James. I am. Currently trying to sew hair into my old jeans for my costume LOL. You?'

I shake my head and chuckle slightly. I don't even want to ask what he's dressing up as. Since Monday's Maths class, we've been chatting a bit when we pass each other. He seems sound enough. We're not mates or anything, but it's nice to actually have a conversation with someone in school when you feel as lonely as I do.

'I dunno. My mate's trying to get me to go but I know as soon as we get there he'll piss off with some woman lol wanted a familiar face there.'

'Come! It'll be good fun. You can hang around with me if your mate ditches you.'

I consider it as I bite my lip.

'OK, sounds good. See you there.'

"Fine, Teddy. I'll come."

Teddy starts waving his hands and celebrating. Throwing the ball at my door, he shouts.

"He shoots, he scores. And the crowd goes wild."

Putting his hands against his face he breaths out heavily, sounding nothing like a crowd of cheers.

"Why does it have to be a stupid costume party anyway? Halloween's just around the corner."

Teddy shrugs.

"I actually don't know. She just likes dressing up slutty. Well, I hope that's the reason. You joining me as a zombie basketball player?"

I smirk.

"Not exactly. I think I've got a good idea for a costume."

CHAPTER 45:

My whole body vibrates with the dance music as I start up the drive to the McCray's manor. To say the place was a manor was the polite way of putting it. With yards of fresh trimmed grass and naked baby sculptures, the place looked like something from a magazine. Somewhere couples go on their wedding day for fancy photographs. The bright lights of the massive house shine in through the slits of my mask, which is already starting to give me a headache as my field of view is obstructed. My peripheral vision is lost in the black of the material and I can only see directly in front of me. I keep banging into people either side of me as I stumble into the packed corridor.

"Oh, there's so many girls here tonight, James. You're in luck. And so… Am… I," Teddy rubs his hands together and chuckles.

"Why are you in luck, then?"

He spins around to see Teri making her way over to him with a red plastic cup in one hand, holding her arm over the traffic of people, hand in hand with some other girl. Teri's dressed all in leopard print with a drawn-on pair of whiskers. The girl she's with is wearing a tight black corset and cat ears. I recognise her from around school, but can't remember her name.

"Oh, hello pussies!" Teddy balls his hand into a claw and meows embarrassingly. "James, you know Teri?"

He leans right into my mask, raises his eyebrows and sticks out his tongue.

"And this lovely lady is Laura."

I smile at her, but then remember she can't see my face. I remove my mask and smile again. She gives me a quick polite smirk before averting her eyes quickly around the room.

"Why don't you two get to know each other whilst Teri shows me where the vodka is?" Teddy sings.

Laura grabs Teri's hand again as they have a hushed conversation, ending with them both looking at me. I shift awkwardly as Teri blows her a kiss and walks off arm in arm with Teddy.

"So…" I say, following her gaze around the room. "She drag you here too?"

"Er… No. Louise invited me actually."

Low blow.

"I like your ears."

"Thanks. And you are…"

She stares at my mask as I hold it up.

"Scream."

She looks at me puzzlingly.

"Scream. You don't know Scream? The 90s slasher film about the lunatic going around killing high school students in America? Courtney Cox? David Arquette? Neve Campbell?"

Laura breaths in, curls her lip and looks away.

"Yeah, bit too close to the bone that one, don't you think?"

"That's the point. Everyone at this party thinks that I'm this serial stabber, so I thought I'd play up to it."

She nods her head and looks around desperately.

"Sorry, I have to-"

She runs over to another girl and I hear her hiss *'thank God.'*

I replace my mask and move through the crowd. When someone gives me a weird look, I raise my plastic knife and make a growling sound. The kitchen better have shots.

After my third beer, I start to make my way around the house, hidden by my disguise. I gaze around at everyone. Undetected. I can't believe how drunk some of them are already. I see Andrew in the corner of the living room chatting to a group of lads and fight my way over to him.

"Who are you supposed to be?"

He snarls his teeth, showing clip-in fangs and flexes his arms, draped in fur.

"Teen Wolf!"

I laugh and take off my mask.

"I was just about to ask how you drink in that thing," he laughs. "A bit controversial, wouldn't you say?"

I shrug as I swallow the residue at the bottom of my cup.

"Don't really care. Might as well give the people what they're asking for."

"Where's your mate?"

I glance around at the sea of bodies, but can't find him anywhere.

"Probably already has the girl upstairs."

Andrew laughs and introduces me to his friends. Some shake my hand genuinely, others flash me a fake smile and glance around to make sure no one else noticed. That's when I see Lydia coming into the room. I quickly throw my mask back on and observe her. She's dressed as a mixture of Little Bow Peep and Harley Quinn. Weird, but it kind of works. Of course, it wouldn't be like Lydia to come in something simple or boring. I'm shocked to see that she's with a guy. Some idiot who draped himself in toilet roll as an excuse for a costume. He keeps grabbing her arm and leaning in, but she swerves her head away before he can kiss her. But she's being flirty back. I'm seething with jealousy. I want to go up and knock the kid out, but I stay calm.

"Hey, James?"

I wince behind my mask. Don't say my name. I don't think she heard anyway.

"You want to join in in some beer pong?" Andrew holds up a single white ping-pong ball.

I get Lydia alone in the kitchen an hour later. She's filling her cup with ice when I intentionally bump into her.

"Sorry," I start, but she recognises my voice instantly.

"What are you doing here?" she hisses, pretending to look out of the window.

"I'm with Teddy. Anyway, this isn't your scene. And who's the jackass dressed as a mummy?"

She blushes and shakes her head, tutting.

"Never you mind."

"Why haven't you been answering any of my calls?"

"James, not here."

"Outside then, over by that tyre swing."

I see our reflections in the window looking over to the bottom of the garden. I use the opportunity to catch a gaze at her. The wig weirdly suits her.

"Okay, give me ten minutes. And make sure you're not followed."

She trudges off and is swallowed within the mass of people. As I'm thinking of an excuse to make up if Teddy notices me missing, I bang straight into someone.

"Oh, sorry. I can't-"

"Watch where you're going!"

I freeze. Stacey!

As I turn my head for a better view, I see her sulk off into the kitchen. My first instinct is to hide, but she didn't notice my voice. Shit! There's Teddy. And she's making her way over to him. He glances up from... Some new girl. Have no idea who he's with now. He sees Stacey and his face drops. Out of instinct, he looks behind her towards me and I wave my hands in protest.

"Teddy. *Where* is James?"

She stands with her hands on her hips. Standing out like a sore thumb in her ordinary clothes.

"Er... He's not here. Why would he be here?"

"Well, he's not at his house and I saw from my friend's Snapchat that you're here sleazing with God only knows who. So, I'm guessing that he's not far behind you."

"Stacey, he's not here. Believe me, I'd tell you in a heartbeat if he was. You know I'd love to see a bit of drama."

She considers this for a moment.

"I bet he's upstairs shagging someone. You're covering for him, aren't you?"

"No. Trust me, if he was, I'd tell you. Can you imagine the reactions? It would be priceless. You're bound to know me by now."

Stacey's head turns to one side as she stares at him a while longer.

"Fine, but if you hear from him, give me a text," she calls as she walks out of the back door.

"Sure thing," he waves at her and turns to me, his wave turning to the crazy sign as he swirls his fingers around his head.

"Man, what the fuck?" he half-laughs as I slide past people towards him.

"I know, she's been calling me non-stop!"

"She's crazy, how did you stick her for so long?"

"Believe me, I don't know."

I grab another beer and lift my mask off, throwing it on the kitchen table as I drink most of the bottle in one go.

"How am I ever going to move on? Why won't she get the hint?" I burp, wiping my mouth on the back of my sleeve.

But it's too late. Teddy has already got his arms around the mystery girl and has his ear pressed against her lips. I roll my eyes, pick up another two bottles and make my way out to the garden.

"Why didn't you bring your mask?" Lydia hisses as she jogs from the tyre swing into the bushes on the outskirts of the massive lawn.

"Okay, now you're being a bit overdramatic," I whisper as I push through the dense bushes into the thicket of trees behind.

"Anyway, why haven't you been answering my calls or texting me back?"

"Because I've been busy."

"Busy for all this time? I haven't seen you since-"

"I know when it was."

"Well, why are you acting strange?"

"Because that night you were with me. But you weren't the other nights."

I frown at her. Am I really hearing this?

"Lydia, you can't *really* think that I-"

"I don't know what to think, James. All I know is the kids from sch-"

"The kids at school call you a witch. They've teased you since primary school. Now, because they're saying stuff about me, you suddenly can't think for yourself?"

She shrugs. We stand staring at each other for a moment, the only thing breaking the silence is the sound of the music and calls from the house.

"Look. You're the most strong-minded person I know," I creep towards her, and for once, she doesn't retreat.

"You're smart and independent and has never cared what other people have thought."

My face is within inches of hers now. I can smell the pink lemonade she was mixing with her spirits. Weird thing to get aroused over, but I do anyway. She sighs and looks at my lips. I can see she's battling with herself. Something I did up until recently. Finally, she caves and kisses me. I missed this. I pull at her tights and she fights with my black trousers. Within seconds we're on the grass. I'm on top of her, grabbing her ass cheeks for better leverage as I thrust myself inside her. Satisfied every time when she makes a soft moan in my ear. I'm aware of the dampness of my knees as they sink into the mud, but I don't care. All I care about is right here under me.

"Did you hear that?"

Lydia jerks up and looks around. No, not now. Not when I'm so close.

"I didn't hear anything."

I throw her back down and start kissing her neck, but she squirms away from me.

"No, listen!"

As my panting subsides, I strain my ears. There's a soft thudding coming from the other side of the bushes, and it's not the horrible dance tune. And something that sounds like panting, reacting to the rhythm. I smile.

"Looks like we're not the only ones getting lucky."

I grab her neck to turn her head around to kiss me again.

"No, James. That boy doesn't sound like he's enjoying himself. Listen closely."

I shake my head as I don't hear what she does. Pulling up her ripped tights, she stumbles over to a gap in the bushes and gasps, slapping her hand to her mouth. I scramble to pull up my boxers and am just re-buttoning my trousers when I join her.

"Oh my God!" I gasp. "Oi!"

On the ground is a boy dressed in pirate gear, I now establish it to be Ryan Meadows. His white shirt is covered in blood. Towering over him is a man dressed all in black, with *my* Scream mask covering his face. The man in the mask looks in my direction. A few seconds pass before he starts running down the lawn on to the road. Without thinking, fuelled on by the drink, I bound after him. But the grass is slippy and muddy and by the time I get to the giant wall separating the house and garden from the old country lane, he's nowhere to be seen.

CHAPTER 46:

"Everybody quiet!"

Trying to break-up underage drinking is hard enough, without the added stress of preserving a crime scene. Dawson has gathered everyone into the brightly lit living room. McNally is trying to talk to a hysterical girl dressed in a Union Jack dress. He guesses she's supposed to be Geri Halliwell, but has lost her ginger wig. She's still crying on the phone, not noticing how loud she is in her drunken state. Screaming to some unknown recipient that her boyfriend has been stabbed. McNally's attempts to soothe her are failing.

"McNally, get her out."

McNally leads her into the kitchen, still trying to calm her down. Nearly a hundred beady eyes gaze at the DI, wondering what is going to happen next. Dawson recognises the majority of them from their interviews. Many of them weren't even given a second thought, then he rests his eyes on Kingston. He smiles awkwardly at the detective, but Dawson doesn't so much as acknowledge him. What is he doing here, at the scene of a crime, *again*?

"Now, I know you are all scared. I just want to let you know that we aren't going to say anything about the alcohol. So, if you're under 18, then just relax and co-operate with us as best as you can. However, as many of you now know, there's been another attack. An attendee at this party called Ryan Meadows has been stabbed just outside in the garden there."

Everyone's eyes follow Dawson's pointed finger as it rests towards the giant window, overlooking the standard white tent.

"We need to get to the bottom of this, so no-one is going anywhere until we get full statements from everyone."

A long groan circulates the room, causing Dawson to demand silence once again.

"So, first thing's first. Whose party is this?"

A brunette girl dressed as Minnie Mouse pushes her way to the front.

"Me, sir."

"Louise?"

"Yes, sir."

"Where are your parents?"

"They're in Dubai, sir."

"And they thought it would be a good idea to leave a 17-year-old girl alone in a house? Especially with everything that's been going on?"

"Well, I'm 18 actually. But I'm not alone. My boyfriend, Kyle, is staying with me. He's 19."

"And where is he now?"

"I think he's on a beer run."

Dawson's chin protrudes as he breathes in.

"Can someone get in contact with him and tell him to come back. Immediately. I think everyone's had enough beer for tonight."

"Why do we *all* have to give statements?" a boy that Dawson doesn't recognise dressed in a Smurf costume steps forward. "We all know who's responsible for everything going on."

The majority of the eyes in the room rest on James, who shakes his head and folds his arms.

"Yeah, he's even dressed as Scream for God's sake," a girl with a coconut bra butts in.

"I was outside having a smoke when it happened. I saw the whole thing," Superman chips in. "He was wearing a Scream mask but ran off. We all gathered around Ryan and then Kingston came running back."

"Yeah, I saw him running back too. But he'd thrown his mask away," a nerd calls out from behind his fake braces.

"Hiding the evidence!" the Smurf returns to the outbursts.

"He waved his knife at me earlier too," a girl in a hideous bumble bee costume cries, whilst others start to shout their opinion.

"Alright, alright everyone calm down!" Dawson shouts, the vein in his head ready to explode. So much hearsay is going to taint the statements now.

Finally, the uniformed officers march into the living room and Dawson starts organising them. The good thing about a big house like this is the many rooms you can spread your interviews across. When everything is controlled and he watches the circus spill out into the surrounding rooms, ready to give their statements, whether true or not at this point, he catches Kingston's eye. He looks upset, but not in the guilty way. For the first time, Dawson looks at him and he actually looks genuine.

"Excuse me, Don?"

Dawson follows James' eyes until the wall obstructs their connection. Turning, Dawson is surprised to see Roberta Mills standing in front of him.

"Jesus, I know you're quick, but I never thought you were this quick! We haven't even released a statement yet."

"I've got some important information which you may find useful."

Dawson nods his head and leads her out into the garden. Into the flashing blue lights and the hi-vis jackets. Failing to find a quiet spot, the pair settle down in the DI's car.

"That kid in there is innocent," Roberta says, closing the car door behind her.

Dawson leans back in his chair, sighing.

"Look, obviously I'm not at liberty to discuss this investigation with-"

"No, I know all that. I'm not here for a story. I know that kid is innocent because I saw it. With my own eyes. That kid ran after him to try and stop him."

"How do you know this? Why were you even here?"

Roberta looks sheepishly out of the window.

"I knew there was going to be trouble tonight. It was all over social media. *'Party at Louise McCray's.'* I knew something like this would attract the person responsible. Drunken teens with no adult supervision? They were basically handing it to him on a plate! I'm surprised a member of the police wasn't patrolling the grounds for Christ's sake. Are the kids who were arrested last week not at this party?"

"Again, we can't-"

"Right, well I'm guessing they aren't as I had a scope around and there was no sign of unmarked police cars tracking them. Anyway, I parked just up the hill," she gestures in the direction towards the back of the house.

"I turned my headlights off and watched the party unfold. Only one car came and left again within minutes, and they weren't dropping someone off. Blonde girl. Normal clothes. Think she might've been looking for someone. Don't know whether that helps?"

"Everything going on *will* be documented, yes."

"Okay, well I don't think she had anything to do with it. But anyway, I tried to make a list of everyone that came, but people started coming in similar costumes and busloads of people at a time, so I got mixed up and gave up trying. Everyone stayed inside, except the smokers. They kind of congregated on the patio, but barely any wandered around. I thought everyone would be everywhere, especially a big land like this. None went far from the house. Except two. James was one of them."

Dawson shifts in his seat to get himself more comfortable and asks Roberta to continue.

"He came out shortly after midnight and hung around by that tyre swing," she points it out, swinging slightly in the breeze.

"He was drinking alone. Ten... Maybe 20 minutes later, the girl dressed as Bo-Beep slash Harley Quinn joined him. They both made their way into the trees there. As soon as I saw them wander off, I got out of the car and started to creep my way around from the road side. I was really panicking, thinking that this was going to be the next attack. Looking back now, I know I was being stupid. For one, she came out of the house on her own accord and led him in there. Must've

211

been planned somehow. But I just panicked! I could just about make them out between the trees from the road. They were just having sex."

Roberta fidgets awkwardly, before reluctantly continuing.

"I started back up towards my car and was observing the house when I saw Ryan coming out towards the trees. I ducked down because I thought he saw me, but he was chatting with someone. The someone in the Scream mask. Making my way back up towards my car on my haunches, I saw the Scream mask lead him right out until they were beside the tyre swing. That's when he attacked him. I shouted, but was too far away for him to hear, or to attract anyone else's attention. Everyone was on the patio smoking and the party inside looked like no one could notice. Then the next minute, the Scream mask was running towards the road. Towards me. James legging it after him. I knew he was trying to escape, so I started rushing towards my car. But by the time I reached it and drove down the road after him, he was nowhere to be seen. I did laps of the surrounding roads, but couldn't find a trace. I'm sorry, I really did try and stop him. But, if you're going to listen to the kid's stories, I want you to not waste your time with James. He was trying to protect Ryan. Sure, the kid might've brought the Scream mask, but he wasn't wearing it for the entire time he was outside. It must have gotten stolen. I think the kid's bullied by everyone else. He's a scape goat. But he's innocent. I-"

"I believe you, Roberta."

Roberta's face is a mixture of surprise.

"You do?"

"Yeah, DS McNally's been trying to make me see it all this time. I've just been so blinded by trying to find a culprit that I was finger pointing towards the wrong person. When I saw him in there, when all

212

the kids were ripping him to shreds, he looked pitiful. Unless he's a bloody great actor, I don't think you can fake that. That being said, all statements still need to be recorded, including James'. We've had words with the girl before, I believe the relationship has been going on for a year, at least."

Roberta nods, eyes bulging in shock.

"She doesn't admit it, so it might be hard. Thank you for bringing this to my attention. Now, can you go and tell everything you just told me to a uniformed officer taking statements?"

"Of course, sir. Thank you."

She climbs out of the car and slams the door, rushing towards the house. Dawson sighs and gazes around at the forensics surrounding his car.

"Another fucking murder," Dawson shakes his head, balls his hands into a fist and starts biting a knuckle.

CHAPTER 47:

I tumble down the hill, arms around my head to protect me from the worse blows. When I come to a halt, I hear the trickle of the River Rong. Making my way towards the sound, I try and calm my panting, taking the mask off. Climbing into the shallow water, I bury the mask as far as I can below the river bed, even throwing a few stones on its grave for good measure.

Sitting on the banks, I exhale furiously. After a few minutes, the adrenaline dies down and I throw up into the water. Sitting for a while longer, I gaze at my reflection. I have to regain control of my urges. I've gotten away with so much that I'm starting to think I'm invincible. The drink didn't help.

But when I saw him with her... Something just snapped. Slapping her ass and pretending to dry-hump her. Stuck up prick just thought he could get anyone. Even what's mine. I hope he's dead. I hope I've killed him. It was completely by chance, finding the mask. But I used it to my advantage. Shielding my identity in plain sight. Once those kids saw me, I obviously couldn't continue. The mask was so hard to see in. I barely made out two faces amongst the trees. I ran as fast as I could, but with the mask perverting my view, I just about made it over the harsh fence and into the neighbouring field when a car flew past. Whether that had anything to do with the party is beyond me, but I ran regardless.

I dip my hands into the freezing water and watch as the evidence melts away with the flow. I bring out the knife and wash it. I wasn't even going to bring it tonight. But I was forced to go. I wanted safety in case someone tried anything. Standing, I wade downstream, knowing that it will eventually lead me home.

CHAPTER 48:

It's shortly after four when the parents' cars start arriving. One by one, the kids spill out of the house and back to safety. Dawson watches from the giant kitchen window. What a hard night. As guessed, the outbursts didn't help matters. Kids that hadn't even seen the attack were convinced it was James. He was still upstairs with McNally. We need to get somewhere very soon, Dawson thinks as he chews the inside of his mouth. A pair of headlights are seen coming up the drive. A silver Clio pulls up and out gets another teenager, stumbling towards the front door. Dawson frowns as he makes his way to greet him.

"May I help you?"

The kid laughs and tries to push past him.

"Alright, baldy? Where is everyone?"

"Excuse me, but this party is over. Who are you?"

The boy tries again to get into the house, Dawson growing infuriated.

"Let him in, sir. That's Kyle."

Louise has converted into her fluffy pink pyjamas as she leads this Kyle by the hand through to the living room.

"Where have you been?" she hisses.

Kyle just chuckles.

"Who's the boring old dude?" he hiccups.

Louise slaps him in the face.

"He's the police, you moron! Why didn't you answer my calls?"

"Hey, hey, I was busy. Calm your tits."

Dawson steps in.

"Excuse me, Kyle. But have you been drinking?"

Kyle lies down on the sofa and extends his arms dramatically.

"You could say that. Maybe a beer here and there. Want one? Louise, get the fella a drink!"

"I don't want one, thank you. Is that your car you've just drove up in?"

"Unfortunately."

"And you were driving it?"

"Well, yes. It *is* my car."

"Okay, I want you to come out with me to get breathalysed."

Kyle laughs and waves his hand at the Detective.

"Get a grip, mate."

Dawson grabs for the boy's arm and starts leading him outside. After he's safely in the hands of a uniformed officer, Dawson starts returning to the house, to make sure the remaining stragglers make it home safe. That's when he sees Roberta over by the oil tank, having what looks like a really secretive discussion with Lydia. As Dawson diverts his journey towards them, Lydia hisses something along the lines of *'leave me alone,'* before turning on her heel and marching straight past him, but not before throwing him a glare of disgust.

"You still here, Roberta?"

"Yeah, Don. I am."

"I hope you weren't trying to persuade Miss Holmes into changing her statement, there?"

Roberta sighs and looks the DI straight in the face.

"Actually, that's exactly what I was doing. As you've said, she's lied to you before. And she has again tonight. She's going to let an innocent lad go under the fire of the school, police and community because she's too self-centred to admit to herself that she has feelings for him."

"Frankly, Roberta. I don't mean to be rude, but it isn't any of your business."

Roberta frowns at him, mouth open slightly.

"Actually, Don. It is. She's my sister."

CHAPTER 49:

I start descending the spiralling staircase with DS McNally. Thankfully, despite the looks and gestures I got all night from the kids, it seems like he believes my story. I wonder if Lydia admitted to being with me?

"Looks like we're the last ones," Dawson comes over, hands in his pockets and smiles briefly at us.

What a long night. The sun is starting to rise over the hill in the distance, shining a yellow sickly light over the crime scene. We watch as Kyle Fisher gets escorted to a police car, handcuffed. I frown, taken aback. It looks like McNally feels the same.

"What-"

"Drink driving," Dawson sighs. "Plus, he's been gone for the majority of the night. He could be a potential suspect. We'll wait until he sobers up before we speak to him. Cocky little prick could be doing with a night in the cells."

He turns to me and winks.

"How are you getting home, James?"

"Um..." He's taken me by surprise. I was under the impression that I wouldn't be allowed to go home. "I don't know. Haven't really decided."

"C'mon, we'll give you a lift."

Thankfully, the ride home is in Dawson's own car, not a cop car with flashing blue beacons. I could only imagine my parents and the neighbours' faces if I showed up in that style. As we sit at red lights, I see Dawson observing me in the rear-view mirror.

"You like this girl, Lydia?"

I stare at the leather at the back of the front passenger seat. How am I supposed to respond to that? I make a funny noise to show my confusion.

"Doesn't seem to be the best girl for you, if she lies about being with you. Even to the police. Maybe it's time to nip that in the bud."

The lights turn green and he resumes his attention to the road as I gaze out of the window, watching the countryside turn to cold grey buildings as we continue our journey down the hill to the town.

The worst thing? He's right.

CHAPTER 50:

"For the last time," Louise says, head in her hands. "There's no way. I know him so well. He would never do anything of the sort. He doesn't have it in him."

It's almost noon, and without all the bodies in Louise's house, it's easy to see that the place is a mess.

"He must've pissed off with the beer money with his friends. There's no way in hell he killed Ryan. I think they played football against each other a few months back. They got on well."

"A lot of incidents in football can be brought off the pitch. Maybe he was bitter over something Ryan did during the game?" McNally can feel himself physically scraping the barrel now.

"No, he's not like that. I've never even seen him in a drunken scrap. He's one hundred percent innocent."

"Well, not one hundred percent innocent. He *was* three times over the driving limit."

"I mean in these recent attacks. Like I said, there's no way in hell it's him! Now, if you don't mind, my parents will be back tomorrow and this house is still a disaster."

McNally lets himself out whilst Louise gets back to throwing cups and bottles into a huge black bin bag.

"Good luck trying to hide the fact that you had a party from your parents when they already know a boy was killed in their back garden," he sniffs as he pulls his seatbelt on.

He's just turning out of the drive when Dawson's number appears on the handsfree.

"Sir?"

"How was the girl?"

"Adamant that he's innocent. No history of violence. Not so much as a bad grade at school. Our little drunk driver seems to be the perfect citizen."

He can hear Dawson curse over the phone.

"Yeah, I'm getting nothing from him here either. He's like a completely different person. Once we gave him some paracetamol, he was very co-operative. Has solid alibis for every night, including last night. Said he got side tracked by his mate having a party in town. Drank too much and lost track of time. I might have to charge him with a DUI and release him. I'm fed up with wasting time on innocent people. The station has had phone call after phone call from angry parents and the press itching for a story. I'm just getting ready to face them in a conference. We need to catch this bastard. And soon!"

CHAPTER 51:

I gasp at the surprise of seeing *her* standing at my front door. She's like a local celebrity.

"Hi, James. My name's-"

"Roberta Mills."

She smiles. "You watch the news? Good boy. Trying to get young people interested in the media is so hard these days. Anyway, I'm here-"

"I know why you're here. Another two reporters landed here this morning too. I don't know how you heard, but I'm not looking to talk about it. Dawson and I are on good terms. My name isn't tainted or reputation ruined. I just want to get on with my life. Sorry. But it was nice to meet you."

I begin to close the door, but Roberta holds her hand out to stop me.

"Please, James. I can't imagine what it's been like. What you've been put through. But listen, I'm not here for work. I don't want an interview. I'm not wired up or anything."

She laughs and my eyes widen. I hadn't even thought about that.

"I just need to chat to you. Off the record. About Lydia."

Oh, no. What does she know?

I thank God one hundred times over that both Mum and Dad are out when we settle in the living room. Roberta's sitting on my settee with Mum's favourite mug stuck to her lips. She drinks hungrily and smiles at me as she places the cup on the coffee table. Roberta Mills. In my house. Acting like it's the most normal thing in the world. But I can't even think about that now. All I can think of is Lydia. She knows. Is she going to out me? Put us on the lunch time news? Oh, God. Why did I ever get involved with her?

"There's no need to look so nervous," Roberta smiles. "I'm here to talk. As a friend."

That still doesn't stop my head from flying through all of the situations and possibilities that could be about to unfold.

"Erm... What do you know about me and Lydia?"

Roberta smiles again, those beautiful white teeth I'm so used to seeing over the telly.

"Not a lot. She's never mentioned you. But then again, why would she? Clara's there every time I see her."

I'm confused.

"Mentioned me?"

"Oh, yes. Sorry. She mustn't have told you. Lydia's my sister."

My mouth falls open. This has to be a lie.

"I take it by your reaction that this is news to you?"

I nod and consider my options. Lydia has never mentioned much about her family, just that she was out on her own as soon as she turned 18 in July. Before she moved to her flat, we just met at parties. In the park. I think we did it in a disabled toilet in a bar before. I've never been at her childhood home. Never met her parents. But why didn't she mention that she has such a famous sister?

"That might have something to do with me," Roberta's smile fades for the first time. "Once I left the family home, I wasn't very communicative. I sent the odd Christmas card. That was it really... Has she told you a lot about our parents?"

I shake my head.

"Basically nothing. Just that she hates them."

Roberta sucks her teeth.

"Yeah. I'm not exactly fond of them either. Look, we both had a terrible childhood. Our mum and dad are both just awful. Drunks. Junkies. Neither of us were planned, but we were kept for the benefits. Social services might as well have lived with us. I got taken away dozens and dozens of times, but my parents always found a way to pull me back into their chaotic lives. I had just turned 15 when Lydia was born, so she doesn't remember the time we spent together. As soon as I turned 18, I moved out. Well... Kicked out. Got a job. Got married. I tried to stay in contact with Lydia, but it didn't work out that well."

Roberta's eyes glaze over and her lip protrudes in a sullen way.

"After a while, I think she started to resent me. She always asked if she could come stay with me if things were really bad. I used to let her, but she turned into a right little bi-... Madam sometimes. I would let her crash at ours and she used to sneak out and go to parties. Bring girls back. And boys back. Come back so drunk she couldn't speak or off her head on drugs. I didn't feel comfortable being a parent to a kid I barely knew. And I was always busy with work and everything. I just couldn't take care of her properly. Eventually, I stopped letting her come over and she wanted to cut off all contact with me after that. I don't blame her. But I'm the only family she has left. I came over to her apartment once I heard that she was kicked out. The stupid bastards didn't know that they still get money from her going to school, but she hadn't even told them. She didn't want to go back. She seemed more mature. Like she had her life together. I tried to take her out for lunch or to go shopping. Fun, girly sisterly things. But she still didn't want anything to do with me. When all of this started, you know, the attacks. I got really worried. But she pushed me away even more. I wanted to know if she knew anything about it and she just assumed it was for my job. I tried to tell her that I care about her, but she just laughed and slammed the door in my face."

She picks up her mug and finishes the last sliver she has left. She looks weird, close to tears, nothing like the face I know so well.

"She's bad news, James. I tried to get her to confess that she was with you, but she keeps denying it. You don't know this, but I was there last night. I saw what happened."

I feel my cheeks start to go red.

"I know you're innocent. And I fought your corner. Luckily, DI Dawson and the Herald go away back, so he believed me. But trust me, you can't rely on her anymore. She's not going to stand up for you, James. She can barely stand up for herself. I didn't see what my parents did to her, but if it's anything like what they did to me… She's broken inside, James. Real messed up! Harsh to say, but it's true. It took me years to be normal again. Maybe in a few years, she'll see what she's doing is wrong. But don't give her any more opportunities, do you hear me? She's toxic at the minute. Just try and stay clear of her. For your sake, as well as her own."

I think about everything she said as I watch her drive off. I feel funny, like my chest is hollow. Missing something. And all I want to do is go straight over to Lydia's apartment.

CHAPTER 52:

Jessica Moore gazes up from her phone again, swirling the plastic spoon around her hot chocolate, getting colder by the minute. Finally, she sees Stacey opening the heavy glass door and run up to her table.

"You took your time."

"I know, I'm sorry. Some stuff I needed to sort out."

"Like trying at James' house again?"

Stacey's face goes blank.

"How did you-"

"C'mon, Stace. I know you by now. Now go and get yourself a latte."

Ten minutes later, Stacey is just finishing her latest story about how much of a bitch James' mum is for not letting her inside the house. *Again*.

"Why won't he talk to me, Jess?"

Jessica shifts uncomfortably in her chair.

"Erm... Well, it might have something to do with the fact that you got him arrested, Stace."

"I didn't get him arrested," Stacey spits back. "He just got taken in for questioning. How was I to know what he was up to that Saturday night? He lied to me, Jess. And his parents. I was just being a good citizen."

"C'mon, Stacey. You know that's not true. You knew he was innocent and wanted a bit of revenge after your fight. Tell the truth. It's me. I know you're a crazy bitch, but that's what I love about you."

The pair have a fit of giggles as a third curly headed girl timidly joins them at their table.

Jessica looks up from her joking and smiles.

"Ruth. How are you?"

"Fine, Jess. I'm still a bit hungover from last night, to be honest."

"Oh, were you at Louise's party? Did you see anything?"

Ruth bites her tongue and gazes at Stacey.

"Yes, I did."

The two girls sitting down gaze up at Ruth, opened mouthed.

"Who was it? Who killed Ryan?"

"No, no. I didn't see that. But I did see... Something... Look, Stacey. I didn't want to have to be the one to tell you this. But... I saw James go off into the trees with Lydia Holmes last night. It's been going around our group chat and apparently someone saw them have sex. I don't know if it's just a rumour, or whatever. But I thought you deserved to know. I'm sorry."

And with that, she runs off towards her other friends at the table outside. Jessica follows her with her eyes, before resting them on Stacey. Her expression hasn't changed. She still has that same half smile she wore when she first saw Ruth. But her eyes... She looks evil. Her mouth clenches into a snarl as she lifts her coat, despite the protests from Jessica, and marches out of the coffee shop.

"Stace – please. Where are you going? What are you doing?" Jessica calls at her from across the carpark.

Stacey climbs into her car, revs the engine and speeds past Jessica. With her window down, she shouts back. "Something I should have done long before now!"

CHAPTER 53:

"What the fuck are you doing here?"

Lydia slams the door behind me.

"I came to talk. About last night. About everything. I -"

"Don't you think you've done enough damage?"

"Lydia, for the last time, none of these attacks are my fault. Thanks very much for last night, by the way. Great to know you had my back-"

"I'm not talking about the attacks. Everyone knows, James. Everyone! About five people have already texted me asking if it's true. Someone saw us. Last night. They saw what we were doing. It's all over Facebook. Twitter. Everything. I'm fucked, James. I'm so screwed."

I physically can't believe what I'm hearing, and can't do anything except stare at her. She's sitting at the end of her bed in tears and I can't so much as offer her a consoling hand.

"I... Er... I'm sorry?"

She stands up, marches over and swings for me. Luckily my temporary paralysis subsides as I duck out of her way.

"Hey! Calm down!"

She repeats the attack over and over until I've got hold of both her wrists. She deflates and starts into a fresh burst of tears. I try to rest her head on my chest, but she pushes me away again.

"Just get out, James."

She lies on the bed with her back to me. I watch her shoulders shake with tears and feel a stab of guilt. If only I had brought the mask with me to meet her. No one would know about us. Maybe Ryan would still be alive. As I close the door to her flat, my phone rings. I groan. This will be the start of it. But I'm confused to see that it's Mum. How did she find out so soon? Bracing myself, I answer.

"James, where are you?"

Do I tell her now or just lie my way through it like usual?

"Erm... I'm up at a mate's in Promised Hill. We were-"

"Look, I need you to come home straight away. The detectives are here again."

I groan. What do they want now?

CHAPTER 54:

"James, why are you back here *again*?"

Dawson and McNally stare at me across the table of Interview Room 1.

"That's for you to tell me," I chuckle lightly.

"I think we need to talk about the Friday night before last."

My eyes widen.

"Okay…"

"A Miss Stacey Patterson has just came into the station claiming that you attacked her on the Friday night, Saturday morning of Septem-"

"That's bullshit."

"Language, please," McNally flinches.

"I'm sorry, but it is. It's been well over a week. She had plenty of time to come and speak to you about it before now. You know why now? Because everyone knows about me and Lydia. Someone saw us last night. She's doing it to get back at me the psych-"

"I advise you to calm down, James. Before you start sputtering out some words you might live to regret."

I sigh and put my face in my hands.

"Look, we broke up last week. I found out that it was her that reported my false alibi to you guys-"

"We knew your alibi was false, James. We would've spoken to y-"

"But regardless, she tried to land me in shit-"

"We can't discuss who reported you, I'm afraid."

"Well, we all know it's her!"

There's an uncomfortable silence in the claustrophobic room.

"Look, think about it. She's clearly found out about me and Lydia, so she's came and reported this incident. Incident? It wasn't even an incident, I don't know why I'm calling it that. It was a drunken thing that got out of control. I never even touched her!"

The two detectives share an uncertain glance.

"We will take your statement, James. That's all we can do. If Stacey wants, she could take this to legal proceedings in a court of law. That has nothing to do with us. So, if it does come to that, what you tell us right now will help your defence. So, be very careful with what you say. You hear me?"

As soon as Dad pulls up to our house, fresh from collecting me from the police station, I rush into the kitchen and grab Mum's keys from the hook.

"James, where are you-"

I don't hear the rest of the question, as I'm in Mum's Mini and out of our drive in seconds. A quarter of an hour later, I'm hammering on Stacey's front door, her mum answers.

"James, lovely to se-"

"Is Stacey here?"

"Um… No, I don't think so. I think she went off with Jessica for coffee. That was a good few hours ago now. Did she not tell you?"

"Why would she tell me? We've broken up."

Her mum opens her mouth in shock and gasps.

"What? Oh, no. James, what happened?"

I stare at her dumbstruck. We've been broken up for over a week and she hasn't told her own mother?

"In short? She tried to get me arrested for the attacks and murders going on recently. I've not got enough time to tell you the long story."

Stacey's mum starts to protest her daughter's innocence, but I'm already back in the car before she can regain her composure.

Driving around Rong Valley, I think to myself - why would she not tell her mum? She must feel guiltier than she would like to admit. But where could she be? The other times we fell out and were close to breaking up, did she ever say where she went? I pull up at the side of the road and press my head against the steering wheel as hard as I can without blaring the horn.

Think. Think. Think.

I can feel my phone vibrating in my pocket, but ignore it. It's my parents. They must think they're going to put me under house arrest. Fat chance. Not until I get to the bottom of this. The vibrations on my leg irritate me. It reminds me of the time Stacey and I had a massive fight and Lydia and I hooked up in her friend Shan's house. Then it hits me. The next day I'd checked my texts and read through the dozens from Stacey. She said she was at the top of the hill, looking down at the town, wanting to meet. Said how beautiful the town looked. I crane my neck, struggling to see out of the back window up towards the giant hill overlooking the town.

Is she up there?

As I pull up at the small picnic area, I see Stacey's dad's car parked across two spaces. But after driving up to it, I'm confused to see that it's empty. Slamming my own car door behind me, I start along the grass, taking in the view as I make my way towards the hill edge. The grass cuts off horizontally as its met with a hundred foot drop down to the deserted ground below. Stacey was right. It is beautiful up here. I gaze over the town and am able to point out distinguishing monuments. The school just visible in the distance. Promised Hill, and its main road I just came off, connecting the town with the motorway. Rong Valley Park, spread out distinctly between the ugly buildings, creeping its way towards the hill's edge.

The city up the road say that our small town is aptly named. Rong Valley. They say we should change it to *Wrong* Valley, as many people take the wrong exit off the motorway and wind up here instead. I stand for a minute with my hands in my pockets, wondering when my life turned so shit. A sharp breeze almost blows me off my feet and I regain my balance. I need to be more careful. If I slip off the edge, there's very little chance of survival. This is where the local looneys and attention seekers come to contemplate suicide. No one ever does it, of course, they just want people to talk them down. That's when my eyes bulge. I have to find Stacey!

Thankfully, I find her a few hundred yards away. She's sitting at the edge, with her feet dangling over into the abyss. I'm getting vertigo just looking at her.

"Stacey!"

She jumps and I almost think she's going to topple off, but she steadies herself. Looking behind her, my heart wrenches when I see she's been crying. The sun setting paints her in a sombre beautiful light. But I have to remember why I'm here.

"Come back from there."

"No!"

"Stacey, stop being ridiculous. Life's not that bad. Now get back here or I'm phoning the police."

"Oh, get over yourself, James Kingston," she says as she climbs to her feet. "You really think that you're that special that I can't live without you?"

She's making her way towards me now, her face a mixture of pain and rage.

"Rather throw myself off a cliff than be without you, is that what you're thinking?"

And with that, she slaps me across the face.

"Oh, hold on. I'm definitely phoning the police now that you've '*attacked*' me," I air-quote.

"Go on ahead, I'm sure you're all on first-name basis by now."

"No thanks to you, you bitch!"

"What? Forced you to give false alibis, did I? Oh, poor James. Such a pathetic mess with an awful life. That why you're up here, is it? To throw yourself off? Well I'd rather fuckin' push you!"

A fresh flood of tears erupts from her as she grabs my arm. I tense and wait for her to give up attempting to pull me forward. Eventually, she slides down my legs and lies on the grass, sobbing uncontrollably. A few minutes pass of silence. Nothing but the gentle noise of the town and the odd howling wind.

"Were you ever going to tell me?"

Stacey looks up at me and sniffs. I bend my knees and fall down beside her.

"I don't know."

"How long? How long have you been seeing her? Was it just one time or..."

I look at her and shake my head. She starts crying again, burying her face in her knees, arms wrapped around her legs. Another few moments of silence follow. I gaze around at the view, eyes settling on the old ice rink up near the ASDA.

"Do you remember going ice skating?"

She looks up in confusion, but follows my eyes and a half smile appears on her wet face.

"Yeah. You were terrible. How could I forget?"

"I remember I was on all fours and holding onto the back of your legs when you were dragging me along," I laugh.

She joins in and we gaze at each other for a minute, before awkwardly looking away.

"What happened to us?" Stacey sobs.

I shift uncomfortably. I don't want another fight, so I can't say half the things I would like to say, despite them being the truth.

"I haven't been the best boyfriend," I gaze out at the view, ignoring her probing eyes. "Even before Lydia. I think I just used her as an excuse for my unhappiness."

My eyes return to Stacey.

"But, you did drive me mad. You need help, Stace. It's not normal to snap like that. Your hormones are uncontrollable."

She begins to cry again.

"I can't help it. I-"

"I can't take it. I just can't!"

I watch as the silent tears run down her pretty cheeks and drip off her chin. I explore her whole face with my eyes. Nothing I haven't looked at hundreds of times before.

"I wasn't going to jump, James. Do you believe me?"

"I do."

Her lip trembles.

"And I never thought it was you. I'm sorry. I - I was just so confused. I just wanted you to suffer. But I knew... Know you're innocent."

I nod and we stare at each other a while longer.

"So, this is us? Properly over? For good this time?"

I nod again.

"I loved you, Stacey. You're beautiful. We had some amazing times. But, yes. It's over. There's no coming back from this. I'm sorry."

She nods and tries to hold back new sobs but she's quickly losing control. I pull her into a hug and we sit and watch the sun set over our small town.

CHAPTER 55:

It was at that assembly for that stupid boy that I found out. I only went to see the sorrow on people's faces. Knowing it was me that caused their pain. But instead, all they could talk about was the gossip. The gossip that almost made me gasp when I heard.

Some weird kid that spends his lunch times hanging around outside the Geology room gave me a funny look, but I feel like I concealed it well. It's no odds if he *did* think anything of my strange behaviour. For one, he doesn't know me anyway. How would he know if I was acting unusual? And for another, he's already too late.

That's when I made my choice. It was a completely split-second decision.

I walked out before Deans had stood up to hush the agitated audience. A plan already forming in my head. I half-run down the corridor I've known for so long. Hated for so long. I'll show them. I'll show everyone. Even if I have to bring down the school and everyone in it with me.

This is my curtain call...

CHAPTER 56:

Dawson sits at the desk in the incident room, hunching over the evidence compiled in front of him. McNally and a few others, his wife included, had tried to contact him regarding this morning's papers, but he isn't interested. He's determined to prove the press and the people wrong. Show that he *is* doing a good job. Show that he isn't the same as ten years ago. Show that the Jill Yates case was an anomaly. He looks from file to file. Case to case. Photo to photo. Desperate to find a correlation.

Gemma Norris. Pretty little thing. Sure, comes from a rich upper-class family, but she didn't seem snobby or rude.

Stephen Begley. A chubby middle-class boy who seems to be liked by everyone at school.

Derek French. The first murder. Apparently got a bit too big for his boots. The students that Dawson interviewed never admitted it, but a few of them seemed glad he was gone. The school bully.

Morgan Brown. A different school. A different religion? A completely different pawn. Or did the attacker target her on purpose to lead the detectives off his track?

Then, Ryan Meadows. Another murder. Not a particularly popular kid at the school. Attacked in front of so many people too. Inches and seconds from getting caught.

Dawson thinks that the killer has started to get reckless. Fuelled on by the excitement they get, and their eagerness drove on from their anonymity, even after over a month. Dawson throws the pen across the room and slumps in his chair. Why isn't he seeing a connection? McNally knocks on the door and pokes his head in.

"Go away, McNally."

"Sir, you're going to want to hear this."

"Are you sure?"

"Positive. We've got a kid from Rong Valley High here. And he believes that he knows who the killer is."

CHAPTER 57:

I'm coming out of Ryan's memorial assembly when my phone vibrates in my pocket.

It's Lydia.

'*Meet me in the english corridor. Room 47. Xx.*'

My heart drops. Looks like she's ready to talk. But in school? That's a bit risky. Especially with everything going on and everyone talking. Then I remember that she shares this free period with me. I always stare at her in study hall. Trying to get her attention, but she never looks my way. Not even once.

She's always so good at that. Completely hiding her feelings. No problem brushing me off and acting like I'm a complete stranger. I guess I wasn't too bad at this charade at first either. But now... It's different. As I hum my way to the classroom, I skirt my head around Deans' receptionist's door.

"He's off teaching, James."

I smile at her and continue on in my journey. As I reach the empty classroom, I turn on the light, close the door and take a seat. Looking at the whiteboard, I see that the class before are currently studying Volpone. I grimace. I hated that two years ago. Staring out of the window into the courtyard, I watch as all the different coloured school bags trot off to their classes. Heads together, whispering. Many unaffected by the tragic death of Ryan Meadows. Shaking my head, my rage builds. This school was shocked when Derek was killed. Now, just because Ryan doesn't play football or buy everyone beer, no one cares about him. It's a sad school, and not in the way you would expect.

I wait for ten minutes and then text Lydia, asking where she is. She replies almost immediately.

'B ther soon, don'tmove!'

I raise my eyebrows. What is wrong with her? Usually her texts are perfect. Even when drunk. Moments later, I hear a click at the door and spin my head around, but see no movement.

"Lydia?"

Still, nothing. I frown and return my eyes to my phone. Probably just the creaks of the old building. Then, suddenly, I jump as the wailing of the fire alarm above my head splits the otherwise silent room. I snap my hands to my ears and squint in frustration. They had the practice fire alarm about two weeks ago, why are they doing it again? I walk over to the classroom door, fingers still dug into my ears, and go to pull it open, but my head bangs off the wooden door. Massaging my head in pain, I give it another try, but it won't budge.

What the fuck? I'm locked in! Okay, don't panic. I look around the room aimlessly, searching for a key. The majority of the drawers in the desk are locked. The open ones are filled with spare paper, pens and one lonely stapler. Running over to the window, I look down at the sea of uniforms making their way into the courtyard and out into the playground. Our meeting point. Some of the teachers are rushing around, collecting the students and whispering into one another's ears. Oh, shit. They look really concerned. Maybe this isn't a drill?

That's when I smell it. Burning. Now, I start to panic. I hammer on the windows, but my attempts are futile. No one can hear me.

BRADD CHAMBERS

They're too buzzing about getting out of class and the alarm is too loud. I spin around with my back to the glass. There's no way I can break the window and make a jump for it. It's too high. I'd kill myself. My adrenaline's pumping and my eyes dart around the room for any means of escape. Without thinking, I charge at the door, but the thick wood doesn't budge as I'm thrown to the side. Standing up, I grab my arm and wince with the pain, but have no time to spare. I'm trapped and, somehow, have to get myself out!

CHAPTER 58:

Lydia stands in line with the rest of her form class, jutting up and down and rubbing her hands against her arms to keep herself warm. She ignores all the giggles and stares she's getting from half of the school. One kid actually laughs out loud and points at her. She gives him a snarl and the fingers, before turning her back on him. She watches as Miss Convery marches down the line and takes register.

"Holmes, Lydia," she sings in her thick Irish accent.

"Here."

"Huntington, Ra-"

"Miss?"

Miss Convery turns to Lydia, clearly annoyed for being interrupted.

"Lydia, I'm taking the-"

"I know, but why are we doing this *again*?"

"We aren't, Lydia. This isn't a drill. We've already called the fire brigade."

"But, I don't see any flames, Miss."

"That doesn't mean there aren't any. Someone might've been smoking in the toilets. Someone might've singed their hair on a Bunsen burner in Chemistry class. Or a massive fire worthy of the Devil in hell itself might've been let loose. Now, if you excuse me, I need to finish the register."

Ten minutes later, Deans and a few of the head teachers are gathered at the side of the pitch, facing the students. They all look worried. As Mrs Merchant marches across the pitch towards the first years, Miss Convery calls her over.

"What's happening, Rose?"

"We're missing kids, Siobhan."

"What? How?"

"We don't know. We're hoping we've miscalculated. I'm on my way to re-count."

"Who?"

Mrs Merchant replaces her glasses on her face and glances at the sheet in her hands.

"From the upper class. Daniels, Andrew. Gallagher, Christopher. Jackson, Henry. Kingston, James. Kitson, Johnny. Mich-"

Lydia's mouth falls open as she returns her gaze to the school. What is James doing in there? She reaches into her skirt pocket to bring her phone out, but she's grasping at thin air. She pats herself down, waiting to feel the thick bulge of her phone, but none comes. Shit! What a time to lose her phone. She stands on her tip-toes and cranes her neck across the crowd of students, ignoring the fake kisses and raised eyebrows from a few lads. Both of them are missing.

"Fuck," she whispers.

She glances back at the head teachers and Deans, still deep in discussion. Stepping out of line, she starts walking backwards, as casual as possible. When she gets within a safe distance, she runs towards the trees surrounding the playground, and creeps her way towards the school under the cover of the vegetation.

CHAPTER 59:

"And you're sure about this?"

Dawson and McNally sit and face a rather scared looking Andrew Daniels, fidgeting in Interview Room 2.

"One hundred percent."

"That's not what your statement says."

"I wasn't thinking clearly. I was really drunk and... To be honest, a bit high. People were handing out weed and I thought I might take up smoking. I didn't know it was pot, I swear!"

"Yeah, yeah, yeah. That doesn't matter now. So, you retract your statement?"

"No, my statement still stands. I'd just like to add to it."

"We asked you if you saw any strange activity or knew who was wearing the mask?"

"I know, I know. And I didn't think at the time. But today... It hit me. I remembered. Like a drunken memory that you don't remember until someone brings it up, you know?"

Dawson frowns at McNally as he nods with a smile on his face. Seeing his boss' dagger glare, he coughs and shuffles some papers.

"Okay. Well, Andrew. I think we need to take a little trip to the school."

Andrew's face goes sheet white.

"What? No! I thought this was going to be confidential? I don't want to show up with you guys, no offence. And I don't want to stand up in court and give evidence. What if there's others? What if they come for me? I'm scared. Look at me, I'm a wuss! I couldn't tak-"

"Okay, okay, kid. Calm down," Dawson shakes his head. "You're entitled to your anonymity, but if this turns out to be another dead-end, you won't have to worry about standing up in court, you hear me?"

Andrew nods, but still doesn't look like he's completely ready.

"Look, why don't you give us a head start? We'll land and you can just slip in a half hour later? How does that sound?"

As Andrew leaves the police station, Dawson and McNally drop themselves into Dawson's car.

"You think he's telling the truth?" McNally says, watching Andrew hop on his bike, stagger a little, and ride off down the street.

"We have no reason to find him untrustworthy."

"But how could you forget something like that?"

Dawson shakes his head and bites his fist.

"Let's just get back to that school before another drama unfolds."

CHAPTER 60:

I rub my arm furiously. It's in so much pain I can barely lift it. I start to whimper as I watch smoke leak its way into the room through the crack below the door. It instantly envelopes the room, making me cough and feel weak. Is this seriously how I'm going to die? In a school that I'm not even supposed to be in? And for what? Coming to talk to Lydia. Lydia! Does she know? Is she safe? Or better yet, is she the one that locked the door? Desperate for revenge? How did the door lock? Is this arson? An accident? I'm so confused. So many questions run through my head as it starts to fuzz over.

My eyes continue to desperately search around through the thickness of the smoke for any emergency exit. But they're only met with the work of students, proudly presented on the surrounding walls. Ready to feed the flames. I rest my gaze on our third-year group project, the Romeo and Juliet poster. The amount of abuse we got for picking that, but Miss Carpenter loved it and we got an excellent mark. It's still up beside the window now, after all these years. I remember her leading us through to her office and giving us swe-

My eyes bulge. Her office!

I stand up and run over to the corner of the room, behind the desk. There's a door frame here, both that and the door have been painted over, but the handle is still attached. Deans' weird way of trying to hide the teacher's shared offices. Apparently some kids broke into them to steal exam papers years ago. But if I'm right, this office connects through to Mr Roy's History classroom. Twisting the handle, I scream in frustration as this door is locked too. I lift my arm but gasp in pain again. Hesitating slightly, I half attempt banging my shoulder off the wood. It's hollower than the heavy classroom door. I massage my arm from the fresh pain.

"Fuck it," I sigh, and start lobbing my foot against it. After a few attempts, my foot splits through the wood. I laugh and ignore the pain from dozens of splinters as I start kicking for my life, sweat dripping from me ferociously. Moments later, I'm able to get on my knees and squeeze through the gap, coming out into a damp office. I only disturb two empty desks as I make straight for the door in front, which hasn't been painted over on this side. I start kicking again. This one's a little easier to break through, and a huge crack instantly appears the whole way up the door. I use my uninjured shoulder to lunge myself forward. Several hits later, I fall through the door and land in a mess of wood, paint and plaster on the ground.

As I stand up, I realise that I was right. I'm in the history room. And there's the classroom door leading out to the hall. Out to safety. Lying ajar. I hobble forward and am just about to reach the exit when something comes out of nowhere and pushes me head first into the wooden door, making it slam shut with the force from my head. I lie for a few seconds, physically dizzy. Sitting up, I look behind me. Did I trip? Bang into something in my frenzy to escape?

I see her when the room stops spinning.

She's scowling at me, lip curled, in her black hoody. Knife in her hands. Pointing it directly at me.

CHAPTER 61:

"You! You're the one behind all of this?"

Clara smirks and examines her knife.

"You could say that."

She lets down her black hood, covering her shaved head.

"But… They knew you. Everyone knew you!"

"Did you really think I would let them see my face, dumbass? I kept my hood up the entire time. Well… Except with Ryan. I think you have yourself to thank for that one."

My mouth falls open.

"Do *not* blame me fo-"

"Ah, ah, ah," Clara waves the knife in front of my face. "Don't get stroppy, now. You're not in control here, are you?"

I glare at her in frustration. I feel my phone vibrate in my pocket. There's no way I can reach it. Not without her seeing.

"Well then, why? Why do this?"

"As if you don't know," Clara hisses, gesturing around the room. "You go here too. It's a shithole. The people in it… They're disgusting!"

"Did you start the fire?"

Clara smirks again and taps the knife delicately off her cheek.

"Why did you start the fire, Clara?"

"I wanted everyone in it to burn. But the fire alarms are well in check, unlike everything and everyone else in this school. I'd say the majority of people escaped. Oh, well. I'll get another chance."

I watch the smoke, slipping in from under the door, break through around me and slither its way up to Clara, like a loyal pet.

"How? They're going to find it suspicious that we're both gone. If you kill me, they'll know it's you."

"You sure about that?"

The knife's tip taps the bottom of my chin within seconds.

"As far as everyone else knows, the fire was an accident. Deans' office is already in flames. What do you expect? Keeping a stash of drink in your desk drawer. Accident waiting to happen, I'd say. And as for you."

She digs the blade lightly into my neck and I try not to wince in pain. She smiles and wipes a slither of blood from my neck up with a finger in her free hand. Her face mere inches from mine.

"Your body will be so burnt that they won't be able to see the wounds I'm so eager to give you."

She presses my blood to her lips, massaging it in like a lipstick. Just as she smirks again, I clench the fist in my good hand and bring it in contact with her face. She gasps in surprise as the knife falls and slides to the other side of the room. I'm on my feet and reaching for the door handle, but she's too quick. One of her arms are around my throat, dragging me to the ground. We both flail about the floor. Her sliding ever so slowly across the classroom towards the knife. Me kicking and punching, trying to connect with any part of her body, whilst the hand on my bad arm grabs for her arm around my neck. Fingers digging into her thick skin, trying to pull her away. The pain is

252

excruciating. My windpipe feels like it's about to burst and I start to see red dots on the whitewashed wall. I know she's feet from the knife, but there's nothing I can do.

Finally, my free hand makes contact with her ear and I drag it down towards me. We're face to face as she screams in pain. I see the hate in her eyes and in a split second, my hand has swivelled around from her ear and both of my fingers delve deep into her sockets. She starts to loosen her grip and I kick backwards. I'm on top of her now, but the wrong way. I stand to turn, but her legs swipe, lifting me off my feet and I fall backwards into a desk, winding myself. I lay half on and half off the desk, gasping for breath. Out of the corner of my eye, I see her shuffling forwards. I lunge myself at her and pin her to the ground, both of us face down. We struggle, but make little to no progress.

"You bastard!" Her roar is muffled by the floor. "I know what you were doing with her."

"Lydia?" I laugh. "She doesn't want you. She's never wanted you. What's wrong? That bad in bed that she had to come crawling to someone else, eh?"

She screams in frustration, but both of her arms are held down by mine, and her legs are pinned to the ground with my feet. My own head is buried in her neck, constantly shaking and receiving blows from her own, but I stand my ground. I shift slightly so my mouth is right below her ear and breathe softly into it.

"What's the matter, Clara? Afraid your perfect little Lydia was only attracted to you because you look like a man? Surprised when she first saw you naked, was she?"

She's screaming, trying to drown out my voice, but every time she moves her head, I follow her ears with my mouth.

"Thought she was getting a man, did she? Well, she fairly got that with me. Think that the other night was the first time, did you? We've been fucking for months. And she's loved it. The moans and groans she makes, I bet she never made with you. And hey, want to know something else?"

She stops struggling and whimpers. I raise my head and put my mouth right on her ear.

"This is her favourite position."

I've gotten too cocky. She thrusts her head back and connects straight with my mouth.

"Fuck!"

I scream as I slap my hands to my face. The bitch has definitely knocked out a few of my teeth. I taste blood and wince with the sharp pain as I breath in. Clara scrambles to her knees and shuffles the last few feet until the knife is in her hands. I jump over a desk as the knife scrapes along the tiles where I was a half second before. Rolling over several more, I turn to see her standing staring at me, breathing heavily. I've never seen her like this before. Then again, I barely see her. When I do, in school, I try not to look at her. Too filled with guilt.

"You've ruined her life," she hisses at me.

I screw up my face in confusion.

"What? How?"

"You raped her, I know it."

"No, I didn't. She always wanted it. She texted me most of the time-"

"She doesn't want you. You raped her, you sick fuck!"

She screams, jumping on the chair for good measure, and lunges herself through the air and across the classroom at me. I duck, but her shoe still connects with the top of my head, making me thrust backwards and her fall to the ground. In a mess of furniture and limbs, I turn my head to see she's slid between two tables, half of her body entwined around a chair.

But where's the knife?

Despite the pain searing through my body, I stand up and search the room. I find it by the teacher's desk and pick it up. As I turn, she's just pulling herself up, visibly shaking with tears. I hold the knife out in front of me, the blade pointing towards her. We stare at each other in silence. Both panting and shaking and sweating. The heat is intense and the smoke is circulating the roof, but we're both like statues. Rooted to the spot, considering our fate. Stuck together in the mess that we've made of both our lives. Despite my immediate danger, I can't help but think of Lydia. How have I ruined her life?

I open my mouth to ask about her, but the door to my right bursts open. Both of our heads snap towards the intruder. There stands Dawson, eyes engulfing his head as he looks between us. From where I'm standing, I can see firemen running down the corridor, shouting at each other and down their radios. I can hear the crackling of the flames and the smoke alarm siren swims back into my ears, momentarily silenced by our ordeal. Almost as if the room was soundproofed and the ambiance was shattered by the opening of the door. Our own deluded reality crashes back to life.

Dawson stares at the knife, before looking into my face. I drop it on the ground and it falls, almost in slow motion, clattering off the classroom floor.

"What the *fuck* is going on?"

CHAPTER 62:

Interview Room 1 doesn't seem that stuffy compared to the hellish fire just recently put out at Rong Valley High. Dawson and McNally sit with Clara in front of them, looking much less menacing in the signature grey custody outfit. Dawson came in fully prepared to break down the girl, but it looks like she's already been broken. He remembers interviewing her. It took less than five minutes. She lives in the children's home for teenagers on Promised Hill. She told him she was in bed sleeping during the three events. She seemed timid and sweet, and after years of hearing about the strict routines at the Promised Hill home, he hadn't questioned her alibi.

He gazes at her now. Her thick chin and broad shoulders. Mixed in with her height, her walk, her mannerisms... Everything! She's butch and manly, and if Dawson didn't know she was a girl, upon first glance he'd think it was a prepubescent boy as well. That's why everyone thought this killer was a man. Dawson had been looking for the wrong culprit. Everyone kept telling him the attacker was male, and Dawson hadn't thought to question it.

Of course, no-one could be blamed. Rong Valley was very rarely the setting for any form of crime, never mind something as awful as murder. But the very rare time that any crime was committed in the town, it was always a man behind it. People in this town are stuck in their conservative ways that make them think there's no way a woman could be capable of something like this.

Well… Not this time. Clara's appropriate adult is perched awkwardly at the corner of the desk. If the room wasn't cramped before, then it sure as hell is made worse with the four of them squashed in like sardines.

"Now, Clara," Dawson shuffles his papers and coughs. "Let's make a start, shall we?"

Clara mumbles something indistinctly. Dawson leans his head forward.

"Sorry, can you repeat that?"

Clara leans forward too and looks him in the eye, the first bit of confidence she's shown since the arrest.

"What's the point? I did it. Now just send me to jail and get it over with."

She kicks beneath the table and slides down until her shoulders are just about seen above the table. Dawson and McNally share an awkward glance before McNally coughs and sits forward, hands intertwined on the table.

"Look, Clara. We need to get to the bottom of this investigation. It just doesn't do to say '*I did it*' and leave it at that. Now, sit up and talk to us."

She breaths out, exasperated, and sits back in her chair, arms folded.

"What d'you wanna know?"

"Starting from the start would be nice."

She shrugs her shoulders.

"Why Gemma Norris?"

She shrugs again.

"Jealous."

"Jealous of what?"

Again with the shrugging.

"It wasn't intentional. I didn't set out to do it. Well… I did. But not her. She wasn't a target. I just saw her and thought… Hey. Looks like fun."

"Fun?" Dawson's fist slams off the table top, giving the appropriate adult a fright. "That girl's life is in ruins. Not to mention the lives of Stephen Begley and Morgan Brown. Oh, and let's not forget the lives that you took from Derek French and Ryan Meadows. And the bodies I saw being brought out of the school today after your little charade. It's about time you started talking, girl," Dawson spits at her.

She's sobbing again, her jumper pulled up right under her nose.

"Look, Clara," McNally takes the wheel again. "What DI Dawson is trying to say is that you owe an awful lot of people an explanation for your actions."

Clara nods and pulls her knees up inside her jumper until the hemline is inches from her feet.

"You said you were in bed at the time of all the attacks," Dawson eyes Clara. "How did you leave?"

Clara stares at Dawson with her lip protruding, almost looking like she's sulking.

"I learned to scale that wall years before this started, Detective. Do you have any idea what it's like? Living in that squalor? Everyone hates me. Boys climb out of their beds and come knock on my door. Hissing hateful stuff through the cracks. I used to lie and listen to it.

Then one day, I couldn't take it anymore. I climbed out of the window and have been wandering the streets ever since."

"So…" Dawson puffs out his cheeks. "Gemma Norris?"

"She was just a case of wrong place at the wrong time. I recognised her from school. She'd never said anything nasty to me, but she'd never said anything to me *at all*. Up herself. Didn't know how good she had it. Only cares about her daddy's money and what it can buy her. Didn't like that about her. Wanted to show her a lesson."

"By stabbing her?"

"I don't know why, it just gave me a release. Made me feel better."

"Stephen Begley?"

"Again… Wrong place at the wrong time. I saw a group from my school and he was the first to slip off on his own. Had nothing against the kid. Just hanging about with his friends. Having a laugh. Something I can't do."

"And why's that?" McNally asks, head cocked to the side.

"Because I have no friends!" she hisses at him.

"Clara, please," her appropriate adult rests her hand on Clara's shoulder, but she squirms away.

"Okay, Derek French?"

She chuckles a little.

"Had it coming. He was a dick. King bully Derek French. Didn't look so hard when he was lifeless on the ground. I actually didn't mean to kill him, believe it or not. Must've just been a lot more forceful because I hated him. Didn't know when to stop. It was in the park as well, the other two were on the street so were quite short. Scared of getting caught. This one went on for quite a while. Looking back now, I think he was dead before I'd even stopped."

Her appropriate adult shakes her head and places her hands on her face, sheltering Clara from her view.

"Morgan Brown?"

"Fat bitch called me a dyke. Laughing with all her friends. It had been a while since my last attack. I just lost control. Was very careless. As you know."

"Ryan Meadows?"

She shakes her head and looks like she's mulling over what she's about to say.

"I saw him earlier that night. Dressed like a stupid gay pirate. But he was all over Lydia. He thought I was still in the bathroom, but I saw him. Trying to kiss her. Slapping her ass. I was ready to do it then and there. I had to lock myself in a spare bedroom to calm myself down. But the knife in my pocket under my costume just suddenly felt a great deal heavier. When I went back downstairs, the kitchen was basically empty, apart from some guy in an awful wolf costume with a few of his mates. I saw the mask sitting on the table and the idea just popped into my head. I wasn't one hundred percent sure whether the wolf guy seen me take the mask, but after the look I got from him today, I knew he did. I saw Ryan outside and put on the mask. I pretended to be some guy. Handing him a beer and leading him over to the side of the trees. Pretending some girl was interested in him. Sappy sod didn't even know he was walking to his own death."

She looks at her nails and frowns. After a few moments of silence, Dawson chips in.

"And that's when you saw Lydia and James in the trees?"

Her face goes dark.

"No. If I had've, James wouldn't have been able to chase me. I did see someone, but with his stupid mask, I couldn't see clearly. I only found out today in school. Everyone knew all weekend. Their smart phones. Facebook and the works. I don't have any of that. Don't even have a phone. Have to use the landline in the home. I saw Lydia yesterday and she was really off with me. Now I know why..."

She takes a sip of water and wipes away a tear.

"And today, Clara? What happened today?"

"I just snapped. I heard what happened and... I can't explain it. I just wanted him to die. And the whole school talking about my Lydia like that? Calling her a lesbo and a slut and all these other vile names. I just wanted them all to suffer. To see what it's like for people like me. People that either get ignored or picked apart. Everyone's a bully, everyone! And I set that school on fire and I'd do it again. Well... This time I'd wait until they've settled into class first."

"So, that's why you went after James Kingston?"

Clara nods.

"I stole Lydia's phone to text him. Everyone was at that assembly for Ryan, so I sneaked into Deans' office and got the skeleton key for the classrooms. When I saw James was definitely in the English classroom, I locked the door. Made my way down to the library. Set a few books alight and it spread. When Deans' office was free, I set the desk on fire. Got out of there on time before the whole thing exploded. The amount of drink in that drawer? I'm surprised the entire town wasn't up in flames. Thought I could pawn off the fire as an accident, didn't I? Satisfied, I went to visit James. But he was nowhere to be seen. I saw he'd dug a hole through to the next room. Deciding to beat him at his own game, I hid in the next classroom. Luckily, he was only starting to break through into the second classroom when I got under the table. Then... Well, I'm sure he'll tell you himself, won't he?"

She puts her hands in the air and gives a slight shrug.

"We have had a search warrant for your room at the home, Clara."

Her face is emotionless.

"We found a black diary under your bed. Care to explain that."

She shrugs again.

"Not a lot to say. It's mostly all in there. I read somewhere that if you can't sleep to write down your thoughts and it will clear your head. It doesn't work though."

"You don't just have thoughts down there. You have drawn pictures and described what you'd like to do to people, DS McNally included."

Her eye twitches, the only sign of emotion.

"Yeah," she turns her attention to McNally. "I was angry when I saw you on TV. Your posh accent. Clearly didn't go through anything like me. Wanted to show you what it was like to go through hard times."

"You drew him hanging from a noose."

She nods her head.

"And?"

Dawson settles back in his chair and exhales.

"Tell us more about the children's home. You weren't happy there?"

"That's an understatement."

"You got bullied?"

"Again. Understatement."

"But you're nearly 18. Why didn't you just stick it out?"

Again with the shrug.

"Just felt like I couldn't."

"Have you ever received counselling?"

"No. That's for the weak."

"Well, you should have. Especially with what you went through."

Anger spreads through Clara's face. But after staying emotionless for so long, Dawson is glad to have triggered some kind of a reaction.

"That has nothing to do with anything."

"I'm not saying it has, but-"

"Jilly was kind to me. The other two were bastards. Don't try to psychoanalyse me and say that I'm like him. I'm nothing like him. You hear me?"

"And Lydia?"

"What about her?"

"Did she know?"

Clara snorts.

"Of course she didn't."

"How do we know that?"

"Because I never told her."

"She might've known."

"She definitely didn't."

Relaxing back in her chair, she observes the two detectives.

"That enough for you? Can I go back to my new room now?"

"Well, boss. What do you reckon?"

McNally and Dawson are sitting in Dawson's office, looking over the evidence files.

"I don't know, McNally. I just can't believe it. A child! And the child of Kane bloomin' Yates at that."

McNally sits open mouthed.

"Kane Yates, sir?"

Dawson reluctantly nods, driving his fingers into his eyes and sighing.

"You never talk about that case, sir?"

McNally had only moved to Rong Valley from Peterborough four years ago, and despite the town being infamous for the killing of Jill Yates, the lead detective barely uttered a word about it.

"Sir, talk to me."

"I'm ashamed, McNally. Ashamed of the whole damn thing. Look, nearly ten years ago, I was relatively new to the job. Maybe two or three years, tops. Worst thing I had to deal with up until then was a guy at the top of the hill threatening to jump off the mountain. Girlfriend had broken up with him. I don't know. But when I got that call that a body had been found, I couldn't believe it. She was found in the alleyway behind her house. The alley connects all the houses on the street for them to take their bins out. Thank God it wasn't bin day so no-one else had to see her. Some kid's dog had been barking and barking. Must've smelt her. Finally, the kid's dad opened the gate and saw her. Rang the police and we were there within minutes. Poor girl was battered to death. Bruises and cuts all over her.

"We found out she was Jill Yates, and she lived in the next street up. She was dumped behind a house or two down from her own. I knew her father, Kane Yates. Our grandads were cousins. I met him once, at a family reunion when we were in our twenties. I told him I was going to do everything in my power to make sure the sick bastard who did this was found. Her mum was a wreck. Could barely comfort her without her jumping. Little kid with a ponytail about six or seven running up to us and begging us to find her big sister, Jilly.

"Weeks passed with absolutely nothing. No CCTV. No DNA. She hadn't even left the house in days. Of course, house to house enquiries were done and the families were interviewed. But nothing came up. Then, a few weeks into the investigation, when everything had run dry, the girl's mother, Donna, wanted to speak to us. She admitted it was her husband, Kane. Apparently, Kane beat her. And he beat Jill. The family was a mess. He was an alcoholic and she was a coke head. They started dating in high school, but had a very turbulent relationship. Only got married because she got pregnant with Jill. He was from a very strict Catholic family.

"That night Jill died, the little girl, Clara, wouldn't go to bed. Having a tantrum. That triggered an almighty row between everyone in the family. Kane went to hit Clara and Jill intervened. He beat the life out of her. Upon realising what he had done, he shoved her in the alley. He was somewhat of the local hard man. Seems neighbours were too scared to say if they heard a ruckus or anything from the house. After he was arrested, the witnesses came flying in. Donna asked for witness protection, and after Kane was convicted, she took off. Hasn't been seen or heard of since. She never bothered with Clara either. Neighbours believe that Donna fell pregnant with Clara after she was raped. For that reason, Donna never warmed to her. Clara was sent to a children's home and I guess she just got lost in the system."

Dawson wipes a single tear from his eye.

"We failed her, McNally. Well... I failed her. I should've followed up on her. Made sure she was okay. Maybe all of this wouldn't have happened."

"Don't blame yourself, sir," McNally reassures him. "How would anyone have known what was to come from it? She could've grew up to be a perfectly respectable member of society. This is *not* your fault."

Dawson stands up and retrieves his coat from the back of the chair.

"Maybe so, McNally. But one thing is for sure. We have one fucking mess on our hands. Almost a decade later and the Yates murder is still causing havoc in this town."

CHAPTER 63:

Mum gives me a single kiss on the cheek and a big hug before I step out of the front door. It's been a few days since the chaos, and the ashes have died down, both in the school and in our lives. It's been made public that Kane Yates' daughter was the one responsible for all the attacks. As you can imagine, the town went mad. People were nearly rioting outside the police station and children's home where Clara lived. They were astounded that Dawson took so long to find out. And by the time he did, it was too late. Half a dozen students were killed in the fire, Kitson and a few of his scummy mates included. Rumour is they were ditching class to smoke in the toilets. They thought that they had triggered the alarms. It was too late before they realised.

I'm half way down my street when I see Roberta stepping out of her car and smiling at me. The smile isn't the same one she presented me with last week. This one is different. Sad.

"Hey," I shrug awkwardly.

"James," she says, giving me a hug. "I was hoping to speak to you."

"Well, you are outside my house," I laugh.

"I know, I know. But I just… Couldn't bring myself to step out of the car. I've been here for about twenty minutes. Just thinking about what to say to you."

267

I give a forced smile, but a tear runs down my cheek. Her lip trembles and soon we're both hugging each other and crying openly.

We find ourselves in the crappy children's play area around the corner from mine. It's deserted as we sit on the twin swings.

"I'm so sorry," I start, hating the tension.

"You have nothing to be sorry for, James."

"I do. If I didn't start this mess with Lydia, then people wouldn't have died. Clara wouldn't have come after me. And it *was* me that she was looking for. Not everyone who di-"

"Now, that just isn't true. Kids were getting attacked long before she found out about Lydia and your relationship."

"But she wasn't setting the school on fire back then, was she?"

Roberta sighs and looks off into the distance.

"James, I remember the first time I met Clara. I'd come to see Lydia, to try and put aside our differences. I only spent five minutes with her and knew she was strange. I never thought she would be capable of something like this, but I *did* think she wasn't entirely... Normal? I shouldn't use that word, but there's no other way I can describe her. She just had a... Manner about her. Some presence that Lydia couldn't see. I didn't recognise her at the time, but now that I know...

"I remember her from the Jill Yates murder. I had tried to contact the family a number of times for an interview, but to no avail. She seemed sweet. Crying about her Jilly. Of course, ten years later she looks dramatically different. It wasn't until I heard who she was that I put the pieces together and started to see the resemblance. Dawson told me earlier that she tried to set a few of the children homes she stayed in before on fire. That they kept passing her between home to home. She was a right little arsonist. I just can't believe that I didn't see it. I thought it was just a fling. Maybe Lydia was punishing herself somehow. Or our parents. Or me. If I had've known what would become of it..."

She starts crying again and I silently join her. After a few minutes, I turn towards her and grab her hand.

"Did you know?"

She looks up at me, eyes sparkling with tears. How did I not notice before? They look just like Lydia's.

"About the pregnancy?"

I nod.

"No. I went to the morgue as next of kin to identify the body and they told me."

A fresh wave of nausea and grief washes over me. I put my head between my legs and hysterically sob, wailing and crying with frustration and misery.

"James... It might not have been yours."

I look up and wipe the snot from my upper lip.

"What?"

"Dawson showed me something they had in evidence. Lydia's neighbour, Tobias Heggarty, kept a diary of everything that went on in their building. It documents at least eight boys coming home with her since July. There could be more that we don't know of. The coroner believes her to have been seven weeks pregnant when she died. There's a large number of men who could've been the father. Dawson wanted me to tell you, to put your mind at ease."

Put my mind at ease? My mind has been nowhere near 'at ease' since Monday morning. The past few days, I've just lay in my room in a bundle of guilt. But now that I think about it, Lydia and I *always* used protection. The chances of the child being mine *are* quite slim. But I still wonder...

"But, if it wasn't for me... She'd still be alive."

"You don't know that, James."

"I do. The teachers said she went back in after the first register. What if she went back in for me?"

"Or Clara? Or because she figured out Clara was responsible? Or because she wanted to protect both of you? There's so many reasons why. The sad thing is, she's the only person who will have the answers as to why she did it. Anyway, I'd better be getting off," Roberta stands and fixes her skirt.

"You can't be back at work already, are you?"

"No, no. I've been let go of the story anyway for personal reasons. But I need to get a new suit for the funeral tomorrow. I don't own anything black, everything's so colourful. I'd look like a right twit."

We both laugh and gaze at each other a while longer. One a small symbol of reminisce of a loved one the other lost.

CHAPTER 64:

I stumble into the seminar and hope to God the lecturer doesn't smell the drink off me from last night. It was a battle finding the room, I don't need to start a three-year war. Not on my first day anyway. I don't want another Mrs Reilly epidemic. I gaze around at the new faces in my university class, wondering who I'll pal up with and who I'll share the majority of my lectures with. A fresh start with fresh people. Just what I need. Bringing out my pristine note pad, I write my name and today's date. I can't believe I've finally made it. A year late, but I got here in the end. If you had have told me this time last year what I'd have to go through to get to where I am today, I wouldn't have believed you. I guess a lot can change in a year.

The school was eventually fixed back up. It was a tight squeeze for a while, only using the classrooms and floors that were safe to inhabit. A huge plaque in the carpark is dedicated to the eight students we lost that term. After a week, it just became another part of the school grounds. Kids sticking chewing gum to it and leaning against it, waiting for the bus. All respect lost. But every time I walked past, I took a quick glance at Lydia's name.

Deans was fired, of course. The schoolboard say he'll never teach again. I saw him once. At ASDA. I was just entering the store when he beeped his horn at me. His smile and eyes were still glowing, even after everything he'd been through. That had given me strength.

The next principal was nowhere near as nice. I got request after request to come to her office. To answer why I wasn't attending my classes. I was seen leaving the school premises. Yada-yada-yada. Of course, the fire scenario was brought up time and time again. What if there was another one? They wouldn't know if I was trapped in the school or not. *Again*. I never bothered going to those meetings. The new office was bland. Deans and I would've had a good laugh at it. And her. Miss Fogarty. I don't miss her.

Stacey dropped the charges. The night of the school fire, she came over. Mum actually let her in this time. She hugged me and had a good cry. We both did. Said she thought I was dead. We sat up to all hours talking that night. Sorting out our issues and being honest with each other. The most honest we've ever been. We still didn't get back together, if that's what you're thinking. She said she was thinking about it, but in the end, I respected her more than that. About time I started, eh? I dated around, but didn't care much for any of them. I guess I just want to be on my own for a while.

Roberta and I keep in contact over social media, and of course, I see her all the time on the news. She did a story about the children's home Clara stayed at. Authorities really ripped the place to shreds after that.

Clara pleaded guilty to accounts of GBH, manslaughter and murder. Been sent away somewhere up north. No one's allowed to know where.

DI Dawson retired shortly after her sentencing. Said that he was done. Roberta told me him and his wife are looking to live abroad once they get the last kid through school. DS McNally has stood up and took his place. Apparently doing a good job of it too. He was always nice.

And me? I visited Lydia's grave every day for a month. I finally passed my Maths, with flying colours, may I add? And now, I'm sitting in my first The American Age seminar, ready to start my new life in Liverpool. I met my flatmates last night, they seem nice enough. A bit quiet, but maybe that's what I need now.

As the tutor comes into the room, I settle into my seat and take one last look around at my new classmates. I could've swore I was chatting to a boy from this class last night. As my eyes circle the room, they fix on the back of a girl's head. Spiky blonde hair, piercings all the way up her ear. Lydia? As the tutor begins talking, she turns towards his voice, and I could swear it's her.

Of course, that sounds cliché. Seeing her face in people on the street. That never happened. Of course, anyone remotely similar, I thought it was her. But upon further inspection, I knew it was just my imagination. But this girl could pass as her double. Everything about her. Even the way she's chewing her pen. Her eyes meet mine and I look down at my pad. Shit! I pretend to scribble in the margin of my page for a few seconds. I look up again, but her attention has resumed to the tutor at the front of the class.

I cough and try to do the same, but my eyes keep gravitating back towards her...

Want to find out more about the Jill Yates case? DI Dawson isn't finished just yet...

The novella prequel '*Our Jilly*' will be available later this year.

A GIRL FOUND DEAD IN AN ALLEYWAY

15-year-old Jill Yates was a popular school girl, but now she's been murdered. With no evidence as to who her killer is, the case is running dry... Fast!

A DI FIGHTING TO FIND THE TRUTH

Detective Inspector Dawson hasn't had to deal with something like this before. Not around these parts. Can he bring Jill and the rest of Rong Valley justice?

A KILLER HIDING IN PLAIN SIGHT

BRADD CHAMBERS

RONG VALLEY'S SHOCKING
ORIGINAL MURDER NOVELLA

OUR
JILLY

'SOMEONE
ELSE'S LIFE'
PREQUEL

E LINE DO NOT CROSS POLICE LINE DO NOT

CHAPTER 1:

Kane shivers in his thin white vest, his thrown-on trainers crunching on the ground. His little girl slung over his shoulder. He passes several neighbouring doors before letting her fall from his arms, getting a small satisfaction from the tiny splat that ricochets through the darkness as she hits the ground. There she is now. Where she belongs. With the moss and the insects and the damp. Sniffing and taking one last sweep of the alley, he lights a cigarette, temporarily illuminating the blackness, before returning home.

The metal bolt of the back gate whines into place as he has a mini battle getting the rusty key out. He turns to look in the window, deciding to finish his fag in peace. The living room is engulfed in the light from the massive, ugly glass shade that Donna's mum had bought them for a wedding present. The reds and greens give the room a sickly Christmassy feel that Kane can't stomach.

"Don't turn that bloody light on," Kane had spat at her on his way out.

"I need to clean up, I can barely see with that UV light."

Kane watches her scrubbing the tainted wooden floor. He glances through the window on his right to see the washing machine vibrating with life, the stained rug turning the soap a pinkish colour. Like her room. He can hear their youngster sobbing from the open window facing out into their small yard. He gazes up at the blinds swaying in the chilly March breeze. Clenching his jaw, he slams the back door shut. Kane charges down the hall, but Donna stands in his way between the living room and the stairs.

"Just leave it now, will ya?"

But he doesn't stop. As he reaches her, he smacks her across the face, making her fall backwards into the living room and slide along the floor, still wet from the cleaning products that are burning into the woodwork. He climbs the stairs two at a time and comes to a halt outside her room. All is silent. She must've heard the commotion downstairs. Pressing his ear against the door, Kane can faintly hear her hiccups penetrate through the old faded wood.

"Go to sleep, Clara. Now!"

CHAPTER 2:

Toby has been barking for five minutes, and it sounds like he has no intention of stopping. Dylan rolls over and faces away from the light protruding through the window, wrapping an arm around his wife.

"Stupid dog," she groans, stroking his bare arm. "Your turn."

"You jokin'? I fed him yesterday."

"He must be wanting to pee."

"He's already outside. Bobby must've let him out before school."

"A walk then."

"It's only gone eight. He can hold his horses."

"Fine. I'll do it in a while. Have to go grab something for dinner anyway."

Mandy swings her legs out of bed and yawns, both arms in the air in a stretch. Dylan opens one eye to see the arch in her back and slides his hands up her top, his old Beatles t-shirt.

"Oi," she laughs, pushing him away. Dylan moans and grabs her by the waist, forcing her back down on the bed. They start playfighting and kissing.

Still Toby barks.

Mandy climbs on top of him, continuing to kiss down his body until she slips his boxers off. Dylan groans with pleasure, but moments later, she suddenly stops. Looking down, she's wearing a face of disgust, her hand still around him.

"I'm sorry, I can't concentrate with that dog."

Dylan can feel himself getting softer.

"Don't think about him. I'm not. Or wasn't."

"Just go down and see what he wants. Please?"

"Are you serious, Mand?"

"His barking is driving me insane. I can't think straight."

Dylan sighs and pulls on his jeans, tucking himself into them as delicately as he can without rubbing the zip.

"What's wrong, cock-block?" he says as he opens the back door.

Usually Toby is very obedient. Great with Bobby and the other neighbourhood kids. Smart as anything. But now, he's greeted with Toby's backside in the air, his nose trying to bury itself between the bottom of their back gate and the ground.

"What's the matter with ya?"

Toby spins around, sprints over and jumps up. Dylan goes to pet him, but he's back at the gate again in a heartbeat, barking louder. He scratches at it, whimpering.

"What is it, buddy?"

Dylan reaches for the padlock and flicks it around, pushing the gate. As it slides open, Toby escapes the yard as soon as the slit is wide enough for him to fit through. Dylan takes a look up and down the alley, before resting his eyes on the ground beside Toby.

"What the-"

CHAPTER 3:

"Come on, Kyra. We're going to be late!"

Helen Dawson plasters the jam on the wheaten bread, the only thing Kyra will eat, before popping it into the Hannah Montana lunch box. Kyra dances into the room, singing that annoying new Mika song.

"Mummy, why can't I get the bus into school like Alicia?"

"Because Alicia's going to big school, Kyra. You know that."

"But when can I go to big school with her?"

"In a few years time."

"Ha! Like I'd be seen caught dead with her if she makes it to RV High."

Alicia storms into the room, her fringe covering most of her face, charging towards the front door.

"Bye, Mum."

"Alicia, your breakfast."

Alicia walks backwards, grabs a slice of toast from the island and shoves it into her mouth before spluttering out some inaudible thanks.

"Wait a sec."

Helen marches over and spins Alicia around. Through the piece of bread, Helen's shocked to see Alicia wearing silver sparkly eye shadow and eyeliner so dark, it looks like she hasn't slept in weeks.

"Do you really think your father will let you leave the house looking like that?"

"Looking like what?"

Detective Inspector Donald Dawson slops down the stairs and looks over at the couple half-heartedly. Upon inspecting Alicia's face, he snorts.

"I've arrested hookers with half as much make-up as that, up them stairs."

"But, Dad-"

"No buts."

Alicia clenches her fists and stamps her foot, letting out an exasperated groan, before storming back up the stairs, banging her foot loudly on every step on her ascent. The detective watches her, shaking his head as he bites into his wife's butter-soaked toast.

"Don't forget that Kyra needs collected at two today, not three. Okay, Don?"

Helen hobbles over in her heels before smacking a massive kiss on Dawson's cheek.

"Love you, hon."

The front door slams and, almost as if on cue, the radio in Alicia's room blares into life, turned up at full volume. Dawson sighs and fills his coffee cup, not yet ready to deal with his middle daughter. Give him an addict, burglar or pathological liar any day, but teenage girls were not his strong point. He'd already gotten Sue through her turbulent years, currently living the life of luxury in some dive in London. But that's where she wanted to go for university, and Dawson had to respect that. Only a few more years left before Alicia would, hopefully, come to her senses, but then they had Kyra to worry about.

Dawson's phone vibrates violently on the table. It's Jade.

"DS Simpson, how are you?"

"Fine, sir. But we need you in Promised Hill right away."

Dawson groans and pours the last of his coffee down the sink.

"What is it now? Drugs? Theft? Assault?"

"Er… No, sir. Meet me at 53 Windsor Place. It's urgent. A body has been found."

TO BE CONTINUED..

SOMEONE ELSE'S LIFE

More titles coming soon from Bradd Chambers:

'Daddy's Little Girl.'

PEOPLE ARE GOING MISSING..
BUT IT WON'T BRING HER HOME

The exciting new novel, expected next year.

PEOPLE ARE GOING MISSING..
BUT IT WON'T BRING HER HOME

daddy's little girl

AUTHOR OF

SOMEONE
ELSE'S LIFE

BRADD CHAMBERS

BRADD CHAMBERS

About the author:

Bradd Chambers grew up on the outskirts of Derry~Londonderry in Northern Ireland. From a young age, he started reading and writing stories.

He exceeded in English at school, and went on to obtain an NCTJ Diploma in Journalism at his local college, before graduating with a 2:1 in the same subject from Liverpool John Moores University.

He has studied Creative Writing for years at colleges around the UK. He currently writes for several online magazines. This is his first novel.

@braddchambers

BRADD CHAMBERS

Printed in Great Britain
by Amazon